THE UNICORN CHRONICLES: BOOK I

INTO THE LAND OF THE UNICORNS

Also by Bruce Coville

———◆———

THE UNICORN CHRONICLES: BOOK I

INTO THE LAND OF THE UNICORNS

BRUCE COVILLE

SCHOLASTIC INC.
New York Toronto London Auckland
Sydney Mexico City New Delhi Hong Kong

This book was originally published in hardcover by Scholastic Press in 1994.

ISBN 978-0-545-06824-6

12 11 10 9 8 7 6 5   14 15 16/0

Printed in the U.S.A.   40

This edition first printing, August 2008

Book design by David Caplan

For Cara

CONTENTS

LUSTER
THE WORLD
OF THE UNICORNS

Forest........ 🌲
River.......... ∿
Swamp........ ⚊ ⚊ ⚊
Hills.......... ⌒⌒
Mountains.... 🏔
Water......... ∿∿

Here There be Merfolk

AUTUMN-
GROVE

0   25 mi.   50 mi.   75 mi.   100 mi.

1

THE HUNTER

ramma, is that man following us?"

Cara's grandmother glanced over her shoulder, toward the library. When she turned back, her face was twisted in a look that Cara had never seen before. Tightening her grip on the girl's hand, the old woman began to walk faster.

Cara felt a sudden knot in her stomach. She had expected Grandmother Morris to say, "Don't be silly, child!" — as she usually did when Cara expressed some unlikely fear. She certainly hadn't expected her to act as if she took that fear seriously.

Stretching her legs to keep up, Cara asked, "Where are we going?" She tried not to whine.

"I'm not sure," muttered Grandmother Morris.

"Are we in danger?"

"Yes."

Cara's stomach grew even tighter. "How do you know?"

"Hush, child! I don't have breath to waste on talking."

Clutching her new library books, Cara bumped against bundles and packages as they scurried through the crowds of last-minute shoppers. A light snow had started to fall a little while ago, and it had had just enough time to cover the bright holiday decorations, making everything look crisp and white. Though it was hard to imagine any harm coming to them in this time of good cheer and fellowship, her grandmother's fear was unmistakable — unmistakable, and catching.

"In here," said Grandmother Morris suddenly, pulling Cara's arm to steer her to the right. They went down a narrow street — little more than an alley, really — and turned in through the side entrance of St. Christopher's.

Cara knew the church well. They had come here often with Simon, her grandmother's gentleman friend.

The building was dark and quiet inside. Grandmother Morris led the way to a pew near the back of the sanctuary, where they huddled together while the old woman caught her breath.

"I don't think he saw us come in," said Cara softly. The statement had more of hope than reality in it.

She actually had no idea whether their pursuer had seen them enter.

After a moment, Grandmother Morris removed a chain from around her neck. "Put this on," she said, handing it to Cara.

Cara's eyes widened. "Your special?" she asked. This was almost more frightening than the problem of the man who was following them. Grandmother Morris's "special," as Cara had always referred to the locket that dangled from the chain, had been off-limits for as long as she could remember. Despite the times she had coveted the gold and crystal amulet, she could barely bring herself to take it from her grandmother's hand. She felt accepting it would somehow confirm that the world was twisting out of shape.

"Take it," said her grandmother sternly. "Put it on. You may need it before this is over."

"Before what is over?"

"No time to talk," hissed her grandmother. *"Take it!"*

Trying not to make a sound, Cara placed her books on the pew. Then, reluctantly, she closed her hand over the bauble. Her fingers began to tingle.

Beneath the amulet's crystal lid lay a tightly coiled strand of white hair. "It came from a unicorn's mane," her grandmother had told her when she was little, and Cara had believed her until sometime around second grade, when she finally understood that unicorns were imaginary.

"What will I need it for?" she asked as she slipped the chain over her head.

Grandmother Morris leaned forward and rubbed her brow with her fingertips. "Do you think I'm crazy?" she whispered.

Cara felt another twinge of fear. *What kind of question is that?* she wondered. Before she could decide how to answer, they heard a step in the hall, followed by the creak — ever so slight — of a door swinging open. It was the same door, Cara was sure, that they themselves had come through when they entered the sanctuary.

Silence.

Was their hunter standing there, waiting for them?

To Cara's astonishment, her grandmother slid to the floor, ducking her head so that it was hidden by the pew in front of her. She tugged at Cara to indicate she should do the same. When Cara had joined her, the old woman began to move toward the center aisle of the church. Cara followed. The pews were too close together for them to drop to their knees and crawl. They moved instead by a sort of scooting method, until they came to the end of the pew. Then her grandmother did drop to her hands and knees.

No sound yet from the open door where their pursuer stood waiting. And no chance for Cara to question her grandmother as to what was going on.

When they reached the back of the church, they huddled together behind the last pew. Six or seven feet ahead of them loomed a pair of large wooden doors, impossible to open without drawing the attention of the pursuer. Cara stared at them the way a traveler in the desert might stare at an unclimbable glass wall behind which lay a pool of clear water.

They waited.

No sound from the front of the church. Was the man still there? Or had he closed the door so silently they hadn't heard and gone on to search elsewhere? How long would they have to stay like this? *Who was he, anyway?*

Cara trembled and tried not to cry as the questions and the fear swept through her. Raising her hand to her neck, she clutched the special. The feel of it brought back an old memory, something she could glimpse only in tatters and fragments. It was from just before she had lost her parents. She had been two, maybe three, years old, and very ill. Her grandmother had stayed by her bed for many hours. When she had finally been forced by another emergency to leave, she had acceded to Cara's pleading and left the amulet behind.

It was the first and only time Cara had had the special to herself. She had clutched it tightly as she drifted in and out of fever dreams. And in that time, as she tossed and moaned on the bed, something had come to her. She remembered only a glimpse of white and a sense of peace. Then something had touched her, a touch that was fierce and hard, both hot and cold at once. In that moment the fever had broken.

That was all that remained to her of a memory that had tugged and teased in the years that followed, slowly fading from the surface, yet never leaving altogether.

As she grew older, she told herself that it had been a hallucination, a side effect of the fever. Yet whenever she thought of the incident, she had a sense of something altogether unearthly having brushed her life. At times she had even longed to be ill again, in the hope that she might once more experience the strange mystery of that night. She could certainly use a little magic right now. . . .

She blinked. How long had she been sitting here, lost in memories? With some discomfort she realized that her leg was going to sleep beneath her.

Grandmother Morris leaned close. In a voice so soft that Cara could barely hear it, even though the old woman's lips were brushing against her ear, she whispered, "We have to get out of here. We're going to crawl to those doors as silently as we can. I will push one open. You go through first. Be ready to run if I give the word."

Cara nodded. Hoping that her sleeping leg wouldn't betray her, she tipped herself forward and began to crawl. The beating of her heart seemed to pound in her ears, the sound so loud she wondered that it alone did not alert their pursuer.

Grandmother Morris was close behind her.

And what of the man who was stalking them? Was

he still here — or had he given up, leaving them to fear nothing but shadows?

The smooth floor was cold beneath Cara's hands. The door was warmer and carved with designs that her fingertips couldn't quite decipher.

"Be ready," whispered Grandmother Morris. Kneeling beside Cara, she began to push on the door.

Cara wedged her way into the opening, scarcely daring to breathe. She was halfway across the threshold when her grandmother cried, "Run, Cara! *Run!*"

Springing to her feet, Cara bolted for the next set of doors, the ones leading to the outside. She grabbed the handles, then cried out in despair.

The doors were locked.

2

LEAP OF FAITH

ara turned, frantic with fear.

"This way," cried Grandmother Morris, grabbing her hand.

They hurried through a small door at the side of the foyer. Inside, a set of narrow stairs spiraled up in a tight curve. Turning, Grandmother Morris shot the bolt in an old-fashioned latch. They started upward.

They had gone about ten steps when Cara heard someone slam into the door. The hunter! He slammed into it again, and she realized he was not just venting his anger; he was trying to break it down.

She didn't need her grandmother's urging to move faster. Heart pounding, she climbed as fast as she could, spiraling up into the darkness, ignoring the prickling of the pins and needles that tingled along her leg.

They came to a small landing. Cara heard a click as a dim light came on overhead. Her grandmother was leaning against the wall, one hand still on the light switch, the other pushing back loose strands of her long gray hair.

A thick rope ran through the center of the room, entering through a hole in the ceiling, leaving through a hole in the floor.

Another crash below. This time they could hear wood splintering. The door was not yet down, but it was clear that it was not going to last much longer.

"Do you have the amulet?" asked her grandmother.

Cara nodded.

"Good. Hold fast to it, and listen to me. I am going to ring the bell. It may bring help, but we can't be sure that it will come in time to save the amulet."

The amulet? thought Cara. *What about us?*

"Here is what you must do," continued her grandmother. "Climb to the top of the tower. The roof is flat, with a low wall surrounding it. Count the tolling of the bell. On the twelfth stroke, press the amulet tight to your chest and whisper, 'Luster, bring me home.' Then . . ." The old woman faltered, closed her eyes. Across her face moved a strange mixture of fear and longing, joy and loss.

Cara shivered again, with a new kind of fear, unlike that brought on by the pursuer.

"And then . . . ?" she prompted.

Her grandmother flinched at the sound of another crash from below. Turning to Cara, she looked her full in the eyes. "Then," she whispered, "you must jump."

Cara stared at her grandmother in disbelief. The question the old woman had asked in the sanctuary — *"Do you think I'm crazy?"* — took on a new and terrifying meaning. Before she could think of what to say, they heard another crash from below.

"That door won't last much longer," whispered Grandmother Morris. "He must not find the amulet. Climb, Cara, for your life, and for more than you can imagine. I have been there, my love, and it is wonderful. Do not be afraid. Hold the special. Count the chimes. Throw yourself to the wind, and this I promise: You *will* see unicorns."

"But . . ."

Another crash from below.

"Climb!" urged her grandmother, flinging herself on to the rope and pulling it down with all the weight of her slender body. "Climb! The amulet must not fall into his hands!"

"Who *is* he?" asked Cara.

The look of pain and sorrow that lanced through her grandmother's eyes was heartstopping. The old woman shook her head, as if driving away some unwelcome thought. "There's no time for talk," she replied, shouting to be heard above the tolling of the bell. Suddenly the rope surged up, pulling her with it, lifting her feet from the floor. "Remember," she cried, "you must jump on the twelfth chime of the bell! Don't lose track! Now go. *Go!*"

Cara turned and ran.

Another chime. And then her grandmother's voice, calling one last request: "Cara! Find the Old One. Tell her . . . tell her, 'The Wanderer is weary.' "

What Cara heard after that might have been a sob, but it was lost in the third toll of the bell, and she could not be certain.

Three strokes already. Cara ran faster, fearing she might not reach the top of the tower before the twelfth chime. At the thought, her footsteps faltered. She was running as if she actually intended to jump.

Did she?

Could she?

Hand on the rail, she spiraled up through the darkness, counting off the fourth and fifth chimes.

And their pursuer — was he running up the stairs now, too? Running toward Grandmother Morris? What if he caught her before she could toll the bell the twelfth time? *What then?*

She was breathing in great gasps. The back of her legs felt as if they were on fire. She heard the sixth chime — or was it the seventh? No, it was the sixth; it had to be the sixth. She mustn't lose count!

Her free hand, the one not on the rail, clutched the amulet hanging from her neck. It felt warm. She opened her fingers. To her astonishment, the amulet was starting to glow.

The seventh chime. *Seventh? It had to be the seventh, not the eighth.*

The glow of the amulet grew brighter. She loosened her grip on it and light flowed from between her fingers, bright enough to light her way as she scurried up the worn, wooden stairs, spiraling, spiraling toward the top of the tower.

At the eighth toll of the bell — she was sure it was the eighth — she came to a ladder. As she stepped on the first rung, she heard a scuffle break out below her, cries of anger from her grandmother and from a deep male voice. She wanted to turn back, to help, but her grandmother's urgent instructions had been to keep the amulet away from the man.

Clambering up the ladder, she pushed with all her might at the trapdoor on the top.

It wouldn't budge.

For a terrified moment she thought she would be trapped. But a sudden cry of pain from her grandmother filled her with such rage that without realizing what she was doing she flung the door open.

Footsteps from below. He was coming after her! And what of Grandmother Morris? What had he done to her?

The bell tolled again. Cara smiled grimly. Whatever had happened, her grandmother still had the strength to work the rope. Cara couldn't let the old woman down now.

She scrambled onto the roof of the tower, then

stopped as a heavy male voice called from below, "Wait! Cara Diana, wait!"

Terror froze her limbs. She had heard that voice before. Where? *Where?*

A cold wind whipped around her. The snow had turned from flakes to icy chips that stung her cheeks. She stumbled to the edge of the roof. Her senses reeled as she saw the white-covered world spread out beneath her.

The tenth chime sounded.

Again her grandmother's question, "Do you think I'm crazy?" caromed through her brain. The old woman *had* to be crazy, telling her to throw herself from the tower. Yet the amulet, casting its fierce glow through the storm, said otherwise, said there was magic afoot.

The next chime — the eleventh? — sounded as she climbed onto the chest-high wall that circled the roof.

Far below her, tiny dots were racing to get out of the storm. Were any of them racing to the church, racing to help her and her grandmother?

She braced herself, ready to jump — or at least try — at the twelfth chime.

Silence.

Fear clutched her heart. Had she miscounted? Had she missed the moment? If she jumped now would she simply fall to her death? Racked by confusion, she tottered on the wall, staring at the world so far below. Cold fear wound its way through her body.

A sound behind her. The pursuer had made it to the top of the stairs. Then the bell tolled once more, the twelfth and final time, and ahead of her a ball of light blossomed in the sky, its color the same spring green as the light flowing from between her fingers.

Clutching the amulet, Cara whispered, "Luster, bring me home!"

"Wait!" cried the man.

Snow whirled around her. The wind whipped through her hair. Leaning forward, Cara threw herself from the tower.

3

LUSTER

he first rush, as she plummeted toward the sidewalk, was terrible. But before she could force a scream through her tightened throat, she fell into the green light, which swirled and twisted around her.

Then her fall was slow and strange, and though it seemed to take a long time, it was a time like dreaming. Afterward, she could no more have said how long the fall actually lasted than she could have numbered the stars in the sky.

Her landing was sudden but soft. She lay still for a moment, staring at the sunny sky above her, wondering where it had come from. After another moment she closed her eyes, as if to shut out the strangeness. Where was her grandmother? Where the hunter, the church, the snow-covered city?

Where was *she*?

She took seven deep breaths, trying to calm herself. After a moment she realized she was lying on something soft — moss, from the way it felt beneath her fingers.

Moss?

She turned her head to the side. She was indeed lying on a thick cushion of something that, if not moss, was close to it. Ahead of her loomed huge silver-barked trees, unlike any she had ever seen before.

She cried out in fear at the sight. Though she knew she had left her own world far behind, the proof of that journey offered by the strange trees jolted her like an electric shock. Only the fact that her grandmother had told her this would happen — at least, told her she was going to fall into another world — kept the wild panic fluttering in her chest from overwhelming her completely.

How was she to get home?

The thought surprised her. The truth was, home itself would not have mattered much, were it not for her grandmother. She had lived alone with Grandmother Morris since her parents, Ian and Martha Hunter, had abandoned her. She had been three at the time, and in the years that followed, she had suffered her way through a series of humiliations in school, picked on for everything from her deep red hair to the fact that she had no parents — as if she could do anything about either situation!

Many were the nights when, after crying herself to sleep, she had dreamed of leaving her own world behind and disappearing into the one she found in books, particularly the collections of fairy tales — *The Blue Fairy Book*, *The Red Fairy Book*, and others — that she had dug out of her grandmother's attic.

She looked around. Was that the kind of world she had entered now?

Remembering the tales, she wondered if she would find an old woman here in the woods. If so, would she be a cruel witch, or a magical helper? The question made her remember her grandmother's request: "Find the Old One. Tell her, 'The Wanderer is weary.' "

Well, if that's what her grandmother wanted, then the Old One, whoever she was, must not be too bad. Now if she only had some idea of how to go about looking for her!

After a moment, she realized she was hot. Standing, she shucked her winter coat. Still hot, she peeled off the blue sweater Grandmother Morris had knit for her the year before.

"That's better," she said, more to hear her own voice than anything else.

It *was* better, she realized. Not only because she was down to her preferred jeans and T-shirt, but because the air itself was better, far purer and cleaner than she was used to breathing. After several deep breaths she found herself almost giddy with the sweetness of it.

"I'm *here*!" she shouted.

Immediately she regretted the action. She had hoped perhaps her grandmother had friends here who were looking for her. But it suddenly occurred to her that someone else, someone not so friendly, might be seeking her as well.

With a sudden shiver, she wondered if the Hunter would be able to cross to this world. Was he seeking her even now? Biting her lip, she turned in a slow circle. Save for a soft breeze rippling through the leaves of the trees, she saw no sign of movement.

She repeated the circle, seeking a path, a sign, *anything* that might show her the way she should go next.

Nothing.

Fear began to rise in her again — fear not simply of being lost, but of everything that had happened this night. Or was it this *day*? Though it had been dark when she had leaped from the tower, it was now full light.

Part of her wanted to believe that the whole thing was a dream; that she would soon wake, snug in her bed, in her familiar, if somewhat nasty, world. Part of her quaked with astonishment at what she knew in her heart was real.

That astonishment increased as she began to look more closely at the world into which she had fallen.

At her feet grew something that was clearly a flower. Yet when she bent to examine it, the swollen purple blossoms, covered with a fine silvery fuzz, were so unlike anything she had ever seen that they sent a shiver along her spine.

Draping her coat and sweater over her arm, she walked around the edge of the clearing, searching for a path.

The silvery bark of the trees had a blue undertone that gave her the same kind of shiver the purple flower had. The deep green leaves hanging from their branches were round, smooth-edged, and nearly the size of her hand — not really strange, yet too different from any she had ever seen before to feel comfortably familiar. Cara ran her fingers over the smooth, peeling bark of a tree. To her surprise, a smell like cinnamon filled the air.

She began to circle the clearing a second time, feeling a growing sense of panic. If she could not find a way to determine which direction to go, she would have to enter the forest aimlessly.

Or should I just stay here, she wondered, *and see if anyone comes to get me?*

She shook her head. She knew that staying in one place if you were lost was the standard advice. But it only made sense if you could assume someone would be looking for you. She could hardly count on that in this situation; more likely no one in this world even knew she was here. Under the circumstances, waiting in one place to be found would be nothing more than relying on luck. And if there was one thing Grandmother Morris had taught her, it was that you had to make your own luck if you were going to survive in the world.

Halfway through her second circuit of the clearing she heard a faint, crystalline sound. She paused, held her breath, listened more carefully. Yes, there was no mistaking it: running water.

She smiled. *That* would give her something to head for. If she was going to find a path anyplace in this forest, it would most likely be near a stream. People always needed water.

With that thought, she struck off through the trees.

The soft forest floor smelled richly of leaves turning into soil. The forest itself was thick and deep, and once out of the clearing she saw a great variety of trees, many with gnarled trunks nearly as wide as her bed was long. Fortunately the undergrowth was sparse, so it was easy to wind her way among it. A mossy substance, mostly green, but with patches of brown, orange, and red, grew thickly on many of the trunks. Other mosslike things hung like streamers from the trees' lower limbs. Above them the weaving of branch and leaf was so dense that only an occasional shaft of light pierced the gloom. Something with bright wings fluttered past her.

She had often gone for walks in the woods with her grandmother, but none of the places they had visited had the sense of age that this one did; in no place had the trees seemed so old, so . . . dignified.

*   *   *

It was not long before she came to a laughing stream. At once, she felt something begin to ease inside her. Her grandmother had always told her that if she was troubled she should find a place to sit by the water, and this was about the most perfect "sit by the water" spot she had ever seen. The stream, about four feet wide, was so clear she could see every leaf and pebble that lay beneath its surface. Gurgling and chuckling to itself, it rolled between mossy banks, here and there splashing around a polished brown stone that thrust above the surface.

She sat down on the bank. After a moment, she took off her boots and socks and dangled her feet in the water, which was cool, but not too cold for comfort.

I wish Grandmother Morris was here.

The thought threw her mind back to those last moments in St. Christopher's. What had happened after she jumped? Had help arrived? Was her grandmother all right? Or had the Hunter managed to hurt her, even —

Cara clamped down on the thought, forcing it from her mind. Her grandmother had to be all right.

Lifting the amulet over her head, she looked at it again. Had the white hair coiled inside really come from a unicorn's mane? Her mind reeled with the thought, and again the strangeness of all that had happened made her feel as if she were adrift on some strange sea, with no shore in sight.

Wiping away the single tear that rolled down her cheek, she looked at the amulet.

"What is going on?" she asked, speaking as if it could answer.

So intent was she on her fears that she didn't notice the slender figure that slipped from the shadows and began to slink toward her. She continued to stare at the amulet until a pale hand darted over her shoulder and tried to snatch it from her fingers. She spun in anger, then screamed at what she saw.

Standing before her, clutching at the amulet, trying to tear it from her hand, was a manlike creature slightly more than three feet tall. He had an enormous head, and eyes that were large even for that. A few strands of brownish hair straggled over a scalp the color of a mushroom. His small nose turned up so sharply that it looked like little more than a pair of holes in the middle of his face.

The creature wore a dark green tunic, belted at the center, and brown boots that reached almost to his knobby knees. His lean arms rippled with muscles.

"Skraxis!" he shrilled. He grabbed at the amulet again, this time managing to tangle his fingers in the chain.

"Let go!" cried Cara desperately. The amulet was her only link to her own world. If the creature managed to steal it, she might never find her way back.

For a moment, the two of them struggled over the

amulet, the pale creature hissing and shrieking, Cara grim and silent.

Finally she yanked so hard that she managed to wrench the chain from the monster's grasp. The sudden release caused her to topple backward. Still clutching the amulet, she smashed against a sharp rock. Pain washed over her like a wave as she fell into the rushing stream.

Shrieking with rage, the creature came splashing after her. Dazed by pain, Cara was unable to fight back as he grabbed her by the neck and began slowly forcing her head below the surface.

The cold water kept her alert, even as blackness began to swim before her eyes. *Give him the amulet!* screamed a voice in her brain. *If you don't, you're going to die!*

But some other part of her, aware that her grandmother had sent her here to keep the amulet from falling into the wrong hands, forced her to cling to the golden chain.

The darkness grew deeper, more solid around her. Suddenly the fire in her lungs drove her to a final burst of energy. Thrashing wildly, she tried to break free.

Her efforts made no difference; the creature continued to hold her down. At last there was no energy left, and she felt herself sinking into oblivion.

4

IN THE CAVE

hen Cara woke, she was in a cave. Almost instantly, as if by reflex, her fingers flew to her throat.

The amulet was gone!

The horror of that discovery distracted her for a moment from the hot patch of pain throbbing in her side. She would be trapped here forever. Even worse, she had let her grandmother down.

She clamped down on the panic. She was alive, and that was the first thing. Grandmother Morris always said if you were alive, you had a chance. Suddenly she remembered her battle with the goblinlike creature in the forest. How in heaven's name had she gotten from there to here?

Where *was* "here," for that matter?

Trying to stay calm, she forced herself to start taking stock of her surroundings. Dim light from a single torch showed her that she was lying on a bed made of moss and leaves. She turned sideways, her movement causing the "mattress" to release a faint odor of flowers. It was pleasant. Unfortunately, moving also caused a wave of dizziness.

She closed her eyes, counted to ten, then opened them again. Slowly. Trying not to cry, she began to look about the cave.

The rocky walls were bare, save for a large decoration made from the boughs of a flowering bush or tree. Below the boughs stood a huge, rough-hewn chair. Its seat was rounded up on the edges, and the depression in the center was filled with moss and leaves, much the same as her bed.

Then her eyes fell upon the occupant of the cave. She gasped, her reaction an equal mixture of surprise and fear.

More than anything, he looked like a bear that had started to become a man but hadn't finished the process. Tall and broad shouldered, he had a shaggy coat of fur that covered most of his body, and a short, broad muzzle that ended in a black nose.

He started toward Cara. She gasped, and if she had had the strength, she would have bolted from her bed. Lacking that, she tried to convince herself that if the creature had wanted to hurt her he would already have done so. But was he her rescuer or simply a jailer?

He bent over to peer into her face, and the un-expected intelligence in his large black eyes made her shiver. Broad nostrils quivering, he put a rough, fur-covered paw against her cheek. In a voice only a half tone from a growl he said, "Garzim?"

"What?"

"Garzim?" he repeated. Then, with a look of frus-tration, he turned away.

Cara pushed herself to her elbows, trying des-perately to think of some way to communicate with the creature. Always eager to help, she had been upset by the look of disappointment on his face when he realized he could not speak to her.

He returned a moment later, carrying the base of a thick branch. When he held it in front of her she saw that it had been hollowed out to hold liquid. The manbear grunted and thrust it toward her.

She hesitated, then took the crude cup and drank from it.

The manbear smiled — a somewhat frightening sight, given the large, sharp teeth he thus dis-played — and grunted approval.

Cara smiled, too, partly because she felt she had made positive contact with the creature, partly be-cause what she had expected to be water was actually a tea of some sort. It tasted quite wonderful. Even better, it soon made her feel good enough that she tried to get to her feet.

That movement was a mistake. A wave of dizziness overwhelmed her and with a groan she sank back against the bed.

The creature made a sound of distress and bent over her.

"Don't worry," she mumbled. "I'm all right."

The absurdity of claiming she was all right when she couldn't even stand made her remember her grandmother's frequent claim that she, Cara, would claim she was all right even if she belonged in a hospital. Though she tried to hold it in, the thought of her grandmother caused a tear to trickle down her cheek. *Where is grandmother now?* she wondered.

"Guh-izz glack?" growled her new friend.

Though his voice was rough, and Cara had no idea what the words meant, she could tell they expressed sympathy. Hardly thinking about it, she reached out and put her hand on the creature's thick, furry arm.

"Guh-izz glack," he repeated, more gently this time.

Then — so quickly that she later decided it must have been an effect of the drink the creature had given her — she fell back to sleep.

When the pain in her side woke her again, the cave was even darker than before. The silvery light filtering in at what she now realized was the entrance of the cave made her think it must be night.

How long had she slept? And where was her new

friend? The moment of loneliness that overwhelmed her was quickly replaced by a tremor of fear. With her protector gone, could the goblinlike creature that had attacked her in the woods trace her here and try again?

Her fear doubled when she heard something move at the front of the cave. She prepared to leap from the bed, hoping that her legs would hold her. At the same time she tried to stay calm, telling herself it was probably only her host, returning from whatever he had been doing.

Then fear and hope and all attempts at calm were washed away in a tide of wonder, as a creature of such exquisite loveliness that the very sight of him brought tears to her eyes stepped into the moonlight.

In shape, he was much like a horse, though somewhat smaller and more finely built. His hooves were cloven, like a goat's, rather than solid like those of a horse. Mane and flowing tail seemed spun of silver cloud and moonlight. From between his enormous dark eyes thrust a spiraled horn, three feet long at the least, that glowed as if lit from within.

Except for the trembling that had overtaken her, Cara sat without moving as the unicorn began to walk to her. The sound of his hooves against the stony floor of the cave was like distant silver bells.

She wanted to cry out to him, tell him how beautiful he was, but worried that if she spoke he would turn and go. Not from fear; his grace and power were such that she could not imagine him being afraid of her — or of anything, for that matter. It was simply that the moment was so fragile she feared anything might shatter it.

She held out her hands.

The unicorn continued to walk toward her. When he was about five feet away, he lowered his horn and pointed it directly at her chest.

Cara caught her breath. What was he going to do? Unsure whether she had even enough strength to stand, she braced herself to try to run.

Yet, as if enchanted, she could not bring herself to move.

The horn drew closer. Still she did not flinch, not even when it pressed against her shirt. Only when it pierced her flesh and began driving on toward her heart did she cry out.

5

LIGHTFOOT

The moment of pain was brief but intense. When it faded, a tingling spread over Cara's skin, as if she were being shocked by a thousand tiny batteries.

The unicorn stepped back in surprise.

Cara looked down at her chest. The fabric of her shirt was torn where the horn had pierced it. Yet the flesh beneath was unbroken, bloodless, the only sign of what had just happened a tiny, star-shaped scar.

The unicorn laid his horn gently upon her shoulder. Then, to her astonishment, he spoke to her: "I see I am not the first of my kind that you have met. Alas, you have a wound that not even I can heal."

The puzzling message came not in words as Cara knew them, sounds made in the throat and carried on the air. Instead, the silvery creature spoke inside her head, his meaning carried to her in a strange internal combination of images, sounds, feelings — even smells — that she could not have explained, yet that was so perfectly clear she understood even the note of surprise that underlay his thought.

"I'm not going to hurt you," he added. "I just wanted to make it possible to communicate with you. It will be easier for me to heal you if we can speak."

"What do you mean?" she asked, trying to keep her voice from quavering.

"Don't speak out loud! I can't understand you that way. Just form the thought and send it to me. You'll need to stay in contact with me, at least for now."

Though the horn was already resting on her shoulder, she gingerly set her hand on it for good measure. It was as smooth as the inside of an oyster shell, and pleasantly warm.

"Where am I?" she asked.

She sensed him receiving the message. *I'm talking to a unicorn!* she thought, so excited she almost missed his answer.

"You are in the Cave of the Dimblethum," he told her. "In the Forest of the Queen, on the edge of the wild, in the world of Luster."

"Luster?"

"The home of the unicorns."

For a moment, Cara felt as if she could not think at all. Then the questions came in a flood. "What has happened to me? Who are you? Who is the creature that lives in this cave? How can I get home? Do you know my grandmother? Why did you —"

"Wait, wait!" interrupted the unicorn. "I can't possibly answer all those at once. Let's start with some of the easier ones. My name is Lightfoot. And yours?"

"Cara."

"What has brought you here, Cara? Very few humans can cross the borders of Luster these days." He paused, then looked at her oddly and repeated, "Very few." This time the underlying tone of his message was not surprise, but concern.

She started to tell her story, but found herself lapsing into speech without realizing it. She started again. It was surprisingly hard to only *think* what she wanted to tell him, and not say it out loud.

"You'll get better at it," he said reassuringly. "Try again."

Concentrating, she managed to get through the whole story without slipping into speech more than three or four times. The unicorn looked startled, and somewhat worried, when she mentioned her grandmother's request that she "Find the Old One."

"What's the matter?" she asked.

"Nothing," he replied. "Go on with your story."

She looked at him suspiciously, but continued the tale. When she was done he said, "This is more serious than I realized when the Dimblethum came to fetch me."

"The Dimblethum?"

"Your host and rescuer. You're resting in his bed

right now. He's a gruff beast, and generally a loner, so he is somewhat disturbed at having you here — though to tell you the truth I think he rather likes you. It's good for him, if you ask me. Shake him up a bit."

"Where is he now?"

"Gathering some herbs to help you regain your strength. I can heal any serious wounds you might have suffered when you were attacked, but recovery involves more than just healing. Crossing from your world to Luster probably took its toll on you as well. You'll need to rest for a few days. As to the healing — do you have specific wounds I can tend to?"

In the excitement of meeting the unicorn, she had nearly forgotten the pain in her side. But his question reminded her of the wound, and at once she felt it stab through her.

"Here," she said, pointing.

She realized that she should have thought it rather than said it, but the pointing got the message across. Lightfoot stepped back. Returning his horn to her shoulder, he thought, "Show me."

She pulled up her shirt. The raw wound underneath was so ugly it made her gasp to see it. The pain suddenly increased, as if her being aware of the injury made it somehow worse.

Lightfoot turned his head to get a better look at the problem. Whatever he thought of it, the information did not reach Cara, because she was no longer in contact with him.

After a moment he turned his head back and placed his horn on the wound. She cried out at the flash of pain that accompanied the healing. Then the flesh drew together and all pain vanished.

"You fixed it!" she cried in delight.

He nodded, but turned away from her. He took three steps. Then, to her horror, his legs buckled and he crumpled to the floor of the cave.

"Are you all right?" she cried. Realizing he could neither understand nor answer her, she threw aside the covers and stood. Instantly she fell back to the bed. Closing her eyes, she took a deep breath then slid to the floor. She made her way to the unicorn on her hands and knees. Placing one hand on his silky flank, she repeated desperately, "Are you all right?"

She had barely formed the question before he was reassuring her. "Sorry! I should have warned you. A healing takes a great deal out of me — and this healing was more complicated than I expected."

"Why is that?" she asked, feeling worried.

He hesitated, then said, "You have an old wound, very deep. It is a wound of the spirit, not the flesh, and not something that can be quickly cured, even by the power of my horn."

She flinched and drew her hand back from him. A lump of unexpected pain lodged itself in her throat.

The unicorn waited a moment, then leaned against

her. "I do not know the source of the wound," he said gently. "I cannot read your mind — I only understand what you send me."

"I want to rest now," she responded, her voice sharper than she intended. She started to crawl back toward the bed, then thought better of it. Moving closer to Lightfoot, she lay her head on his side and sighed. The loss of her parents was something she did not talk about. Never. Not with anyone.

With a skill born of long practice, she pushed her secret sorrows to the back of her mind and slept.

She was woken by something pulling her hair.

Before she could force her eyes open she heard Lightfoot whicker. A small voice chattered an indignant reply.

Now she did manage to open her eyes.

Crouching near her was a creature just over a foot high. It looked like a cross between a monkey and a squirrel. It had thick fur that grew in two shades of gray, dark on its head and back, lighter on its face, limbs, and stomach. Its bushy tail flicked back and forth as it stared at her from enormous eyes that seemed much too large for its face. Those eyes — dark, with bright blue pupils — were lively and intelligent.

Cara was accustomed to small animals being timid around humans, so she was startled when the gray creature skittered up to her face. Extending a three-fingered hand, it touched her cheek, then rubbed it with its thumb.

"Don't be frightened," Lightfoot told her. "He's harmless. Annoying, but harmless."

"What . . . who is he?" she thought.

"The Squijum."

Cara reached toward the little creature. When her hand made contact with him, he blinked but did not run. His fur was soft and warm.

"*The* Squijum?" she thought to Lightfoot. "Does that mean he's the only one?"

"As far as I know."

"If he's the only one, where did he come from?"

"I don't have the slightest idea," replied the unicorn. "And I'm sure I don't care," he added pointedly.

The Squijum turned his head and chittered at Lightfoot. Even without her connection to Lightfoot, his indignation would have been clear to Cara. *With* the connection, she understood him to be saying something along the lines of, "Mean hornhead not love good Squijum phooey bad hotcha!"

Lightfoot snorted in response.

Suddenly a shadow stretched over them. With a screech the Squijum scrambled over Cara's side and cowered behind her.

Cara turned to look over her shoulder. For a moment her heart leaped in horror. Almost as quickly, she felt a surge of relief. The creature standing at the entrance of the cave was the one she had seen the first time she woke here — the Dimblethum. She wondered if he, too, was the only one of his kind.

He appeared to be smiling, though it wasn't easy to tell, given his bearlike face. Holding up a big, furry paw, he said, "The Dimblethum has something that belongs to you."

6

THE QUEEN'S AMULETS

"The amulet!" cried Cara. "Where did you find it?"

The Dimblethum looked at Lightfoot, who made some noises in his throat. With a shock, Cara realized that he was repeating her words, translating them for the Dimblethum. But it made sense; just because her connection to Lightfoot let her understand the Dimblethum, there was no reason to expect that *he* would be able to understand *her*.

When Lightfoot was done translating, the Dimblethum made a sound deep in his throat that she took to be a chuckle. "Old Dimblethum has his ways," he said. Crossing to where she sat beside Lightfoot, he dropped the amulet into her lap.

She picked it up with her free hand, then cried out in sorrow when she realized that the golden chain had been broken.

"Peace," said Lightfoot. "Chains can be mended. It is enough that we have it back."

Blushing at the rebuke, Cara turned to the Dimblethum and said, "Thank you." Lightfoot translated for her. The manbear nodded and made a growl of acceptance.

"How did you get it back from the delver?" the unicorn asked, echoing Cara's earlier question. He spoke aloud for the Dimblethum's sake, at the same time sending the message to Cara. From the picture that formed in her mind, she understood that by "delver" he meant the creature that had attacked her in the woods.

The Dimblethum chuckled again. "Friends of the Dimblethum followed delver through the forest. Friends of the Dimblethum kept watch, kept track, kept hot on trail. Friends of the Dimblethum showed the way. Easy to follow delver. Easy to crunch delver, bring back amulet."

Now the creature scowled and held out his big hand in a gesture that Cara understood to mean that he wanted her to hand him the amulet. Broken chain dangling over his furry fingers, he held it up and said, "What is not easy is what to do next. This cannot stay here."

"Why not?" asked Lightfoot.

"Look carefully. This is one of the five."

"Hotcha!" cried the Squijum, running up the Dimblethum's side as if he were climbing a tree. "Let's see, let's see!"

The Dimblethum plucked the Squijum from his side and dropped him to the floor.

"Want to see!" he sputtered. But he stayed where he had landed — at least until the Dimblethum held the amulet before Lightfoot. Then he scurried underneath the larger creature and looked up eagerly.

After a moment the unicorn sighed. "You're right, it *is* one of the five."

"What are you talking about?" asked Cara.

Lightfoot closed his eyes. "Many centuries ago the Queen ordered the creation of five amulets to be used as rewards for those who had given great service to Luster. The wisdom of this decision is still much argued, for the special property of these amulets was that under the right circumstances they would let the bearer pass between Earth and Luster without going through one of the main gates. This is a great power. Like most great powers, it carries the possibility for great mischief. How did you come by this amulet, anyway?"

"My grandmother gave it to me."

"Who is your grandmother?" asked the unicorn curiously.

"Her name is Ivy Morris."

"That sounds familiar," he said after a moment. "I suppose I should have paid more attention in history."

Cara was trying to take in the idea that her grand-mother had done something important in the history of this world when the Dimblethum growled, "The amulet must go to the Queen."

"Wait a minute," Cara objected. "My grandmother told me to find the 'Old One.' *That's* where I want to go. And the amulet stays with me!"

At once she wondered if she would make the others angry. But Lightfoot actually laughed — a beautiful, bell-like sound.

"What's so funny?" she demanded.

"One of the Queen's many names is the 'Old One.' So the Dimblethum is suggesting the same thing your grandmother wanted." He sighed, then added, "Unfortunately, I think the Dimblethum is right."

"Of course the Dimblethum is right!" growled that creature. "If this amulet falls into the wrong hands — "

He broke off, shaking his head at the thought.

"I can help; I can guide!" chittered the Squijum.

Lightfoot's response to the little creature's claims was a derisive snort.

"Small and fast!" the squijum chittered, scampering around the Dimblethum's feet. "Small and fast, can look and find! Want to go! Hotcha!"

"If I say no, I suppose you'll follow us anyway," said Lightfoot.

"Yes! Yes! Glorious yes!" he cried, hugging his tail.

"How about you?" Lightfoot asked, turning to the Dimblethum. "If we go to the Queen, will you accompany us?"

The creature made a series of whuffles and growls that translated to: "The Dimblethum will come part of the way with you. But despite your friendship with him, you know he has little love for your kind, invaders that you are. He will not enter the court of the Queen."

"Invaders?" Cara thought to Lightfoot.

"I will explain later," he replied.

Once it was decided that they were to carry the amulet to the Queen, the conference quickly ended. It was clear that the Dimblethum was not the sort to sit around and chat; decision made, he was ready to leave. And since there was nothing to pack, no relatives to notify, no mail to cancel, there was not much for it but to get up and go. However, therein lay the problem: Both Cara and Lightfoot were still too weak to travel.

"Tomorrow morning, at first light," promised the unicorn. "I'll be ready then."

The Dimblethum made an unhappy noise deep in his throat. "The longer we stay here, the more apt the delvers are to come for us. They will be mad that the Dimblethum took the amulet back. The Dimblethum is more than a match for three or four of them. If they send more, the Dimblethum and his friends could be in trouble."

"We'll be in as much trouble if we try to travel too soon," replied Lightfoot. "Both the child and I will slow things down, and make us easy targets. By morning I will be at full strength, and can even carry her if necessary."

The Dimblethum grumbled but admitted the sense in this. Scooping Cara into his great arms, he deposited her in the bed once more. He roamed restlessly about the cave for a while and finally went back out into the night.

Once he was gone, Lightfoot knelt beside Cara's bed. She placed her hand on his shoulder.

"I have so many questions!" she thought to him.

"My mother says I have an answer for everything," he replied, sounding amused. "Of course, she also claims most of them are neither right nor wise. But I'll do what I can."

"Where is your mother?" asked Cara. She had a thousand other questions, all of them more pressing. But her sudden sense that the unicorn was perhaps not as old as she had first thought, combined with her own interest in missing mothers, pushed the other questions aside.

"She is at Summerhaven," said Lightfoot. "With the Queen."

Cara detected a note of uneasiness beneath his light tone. Remembering his earlier comment about it being unfortunate that the Dimblethum was right, she said, "You don't really want to go there, do you?"

"I don't want to talk about it," he replied sharply. "When you said you had questions, I didn't realize they were all going to be about me!"

Cara lifted her hand from his shoulder, a little

surprised that he could be so testy. After a moment she tried again. "Why did the Dimblethum call you invaders?"

Lightfoot sighed. "My friend does not like it that we unicorns came here from Earth. Actually, I don't think he minds *us* so much as the fact that in opening gates between Earth and Luster we made it possible for *others* to enter here as well. He holds the unicorns responsible for everyone who has come here as a result — including the delvers." He paused, then said, "Also, I think something happened between the Dimblethum and the Queen. Unfortunately, I've never been able to get that story."

"Is the Queen a unicorn or a human?" asked Cara.

Lightfoot snorted at the idea that the Queen might be a human. "Her name is Arabella Skydancer," he said, "and she is the oldest and the wisest of our kind. Unfortunately, she is thinning now. Sometimes you can see right through her."

"Thinning?"

An uncomfortable silence fell between them. After a moment Lightfoot muttered, "I have said more than I should."

Cara clenched her jaw. She hated that kind of half secret.

"How far away is the Queen?" she asked, looking for a question that Lightfoot *would* answer.

"Many days. How many depends partly on how fast you can travel — that, and how much trouble we have along the way."

"Are you expecting trouble?"

"It depends on what the delvers are up to."

"Tell me about the delvers."

"Nasty creatures," replied Lightfoot. She could feel his flesh shiver beneath her fingers. "They live underground, and they are the sworn enemies of the unicorns."

His message didn't come precisely in words, of course; part of it was an *image* of a delver.

"Why are they your enemies?" asked Cara.

"Many reasons," replied Lightfoot. He paused, then added, "Our path will take us to Grimwold's Cavern. Perhaps he will tell you more about them."

"Grimwold?"

"He is the Keeper of the Unicorn Chronicles, and he knows more stories than anyone in the world. However, right now I am only interested in one story, and that is the one in which we are caught. In that story, the only clever thing for either of us to do is get some rest so we will be ready to travel in the morning."

Cara began to protest. Her mind was spinning with a thousand more questions. But she had already pushed herself further than she should, and her body was insisting that she sleep. No amount of curiosity was able to overcome that need.

Lying back, she quickly fell into a deep slumber, waking only when the Dimblethum returned with leaves and berries. She watched as he brewed some tea, which he brought to her in one of his wooden cups. Remembering the last drink he had served her, she took an eager sip.

"Gack!" she cried. "This is terrible!"

Making a face, she tried to hand the cup back to him.

He growled, which made her flinch, even though by now she understood that the sound was more likely to be the Dimblethum's version of speech than an actual danger sign.

Resting his horn on her shoulder, Lightfoot said, "Drink it. It will help you regain your strength — which you're going to need."

Cara grimaced but took the cup back from the Dimblethum and downed the entire brew. When she was finished she rubbed her hand over her mouth and said bitterly, "That's worse than the stuff Grandmother Morris gives me when I'm sick."

The thought of her grandmother sent a wave of worry washing through her. Again — as she would often in the days to come — she wondered if the old woman had escaped the man who had been chasing them.

"Go back to sleep," Lightfoot told her. "We travel at first light, and you need all the rest you can get."

She closed her eyes but did not sleep. Now that the edge of her exhaustion had been dulled, the questions and fears that filled her mind came to the fore again. She was impossibly far from home, from her grandmother, from everything she had ever known and loved, and she had no idea whether she would ever see any of them again. A tear trickled from the corner of her eye.

She lay still in the darkness, looking into the darkness inside, fighting back the memory of her earliest loss, the most painful one of all. The hurt was still strong, after all these years. After a time it merged in her mind with her last afternoon on Earth and the terrifying pursuit in the church. She slipped into a fever dream as her imagination kept struggling and failing to form the face of the man who had chased them. She cried out into the darkness, certain that if she could only see that face, it would solve a great riddle for her.

7

JOURNEY

The Forest of the Queen, Cara decided, must go on forever. They had been traveling since first light, and nothing seemed to have changed. The trees still stretched as far as she could see in every direction — not that she could see very far.

It didn't bother her, really. She loved being in the woods, and now that she had Lightfoot, the Dimblethum, and the Squijum for company, she felt neither as lonely nor as frightened as she had the day before. Her mood was helped by the forest itself, which was deeply beautiful, filled with great trees, mossy boulders, and babbling brooks. Brightly colored birds flew overhead, and butterflies floated in the few shafts of sunlight that managed to pierce the forest canopy.

Oddly, her worst moments came when she saw the most beautiful sights. Before she could block the thought, she would think, *I wish Gramma could see this!* — which would immediately make her aware of how far from home she was and of her concern for her grandmother.

At those times she would wrap her hand around the amulet, and holding it tight, think, *I'll come back to you, Grandmother! I won't leave you!* She meant it; she knew too well what it was like to be abandoned.

Though the Dimblethum appeared to be lumbering along, he moved with a speed and silence that — given his size — was astonishing to Cara. As for the Squijum, he kept scampering ahead, disappearing from sight, then racing up from behind them. He was forever skittering up the trunk of one tree and zipping back down another, and twice Cara saw him make a long leap from one branch to another. She caught her breath at the sight. Though it was no more than she had seen squirrels do at home, watching a creature she had actually spoken to do it made the stunt seem vastly more daring.

Cara had started out walking, but after an hour she found herself stumbling and dizzy. The second time she tripped over a root, Lightfoot knelt and told her to climb on his back. She was thrilled at the thought of riding a unicorn but a little worried as well. It felt not properly respectful — a little like blowing bubblegum in church.

"It would certainly astonish Moonheart to hear you say that," Lightfoot responded, when she expressed her concern.

"Who is Moonheart?"

Lightfoot snorted. "My uncle. He's also one of the crankier unicorns you are apt to meet. I don't think he can imagine anyone feeling a need to show *me* respect."

This talk of uncles and respect prompted Cara to ask something else she had been wondering: "How old *are* you, anyway?"

"Old by your terms, quite young by ours."

"What does that mean?"

"Specifically? It means that even though I am slightly over a hundred years old, Moonheart and the others treat me as if I were what you would call 'a teenager.'"

"How do you know about things like teenagers?" she asked in surprise.

"Oh, we watch your world fairly carefully. Look out — low branch coming up."

Cara ducked as they passed under the branch. Her long red hair spilled forward so that it draped across Lightfoot's shoulder, looking like wine on white silk.

Since she was not speaking aloud, it was perfectly easy to carry on the conversation while she was bent low to his neck. "How do you watch our world?" she asked. "And *why*?"

"You make us nervous," he replied. "The unicorn hunters — who drove us from Earth to begin with — have not forgotten us. They are forever trying to find a way to come here. That is one reason the amulets are so dangerous."

"There are still people on Earth who hunt unicorns?" she asked in surprise. "I thought everyone believed you were imaginary." She blushed, wondering if she had insulted him.

"That's what we would like them to think," he replied. "But there are some who know the truth, some friends, some enemies."

She felt a sense of embarrassment at coming from a species that had hunted unicorns, and wished that she could separate herself from the brutality of the idea. She decided to change the subject.

"What did you mean when you said that you were not the first of your kind that I had met?" she asked.

"Don't you remember?" he asked in surprise.

"Maybe I do," she said slowly. "Was it when I was very little?"

"I don't know. I simply know that I could tell that I was not the first unicorn to heal you."

"I knew it!" she cried. "I always thought I had been visited by a unicorn when I was little. But after a while people convinced me that I must have been imagining it."

"It's just as well," he replied. "As I said, we prefer people to believe we don't exist."

She had more questions, but just then their path led them by a narrow waterfall that wavered down the face of a cliff towering at least a thousand feet above them. At the base of the fall was a pool, from which ran a stream that crossed their path.

"Hold tight," said Lightfoot. Before Cara had a chance to ask why, he started to run, then leaped nimbly over the stream. The Dimblethum splashed through, grumbling to himself as he went. The Squijum crossed by climbing a tree and leaping from its branches to those of a tree on the other side.

A clearing bordered the pool on this side of the stream, and they decided to stop for a rest. Lightfoot nibbled pale green flowers from a vine that grew at the edge of the trees. The Dimblethum pointed to some berries and with a nod indicated that Cara should eat them. She was more than happy to oblige and even happier when they exploded in her mouth with a burst of flavor sweeter and tangier than any she had experienced at home.

The Dimblethum started to pick berries from a spot close by her side. Looking up at his towering presence, Cara wondered if he was standing so close to be sociable, or if he was there to protect her. Either way, she was glad of his presence. She wished very much that she could talk to him.

Having eaten her fill, she found herself thirsty. She looked at the stream, wondering if it was safe to drink from it. Unable to ask the Dimblethum, she went to Lightfoot and placed her hand on his shoulder.

"I'm thirsty."

"Wait until I clear the water."

"What do you mean?"

"It's one of our tricks," he replied, and this time she felt a bit of a chuckle beneath the answer. Walking lightly across the grass, he knelt at the edge of the pool and lowered his horn so that the tip was immersed in the water.

Cara hurried over to stand beside him.

The surface of the pond seemed to tremble as rays of silver extended from Lightfoot's horn across the water — though whether they were a reflection of the horn, or something stranger, Cara could not say for sure.

In the center of the pond a large fish broke the surface, leaped twisting and golden into the air, then returned to the water with a loud *smack!*

A moment later Lightfoot stood and shook his head, spattering silver water in all directions.

Cara put her hand on his shoulder.

"Safe to drink," he thought to her. "Actually, it was all right before I did that, though I couldn't have been certain until I tried it. Anyway, it will taste better now."

"Thank you," she replied.

Kneeling, she cupped her hands in the water, which was crystal clear, and lifted some to her lips. It was like drinking diamonds. She drank more, dipping her hands greedily into the stream. When she was full, more than full, she rinsed her face and turned to Lightfoot to ask him what he had done to the water.

Before she could speak, the Squijum began to shriek.

Lightfoot spun, reared on his hind legs, trumpeted in anger. The Dimblethum began to roar. Cara slipped her hand into her pocket and clutched the amulet.

8

DELVERS

band of delvers — at least a dozen of them — stood in the shadows at the edge of the clearing. Each was holding a spear topped by a wicked-looking metal point.

Cara held her breath. Even if her friends managed to stand against these numbers — which seemed unlikely — she could not imagine them coming through the battle unscathed. She began to tremble. Though she had only known them for a day, the idea of any of them being hurt was more than she could bear. She tried to force her mind to erase the terrible images it was creating, images of Light-foot being speared by a delver, falling, bleeding. . . .

Stop it! she told herself. *You have to be ready to help.*

The thought astonished her. How could *she* help in the fight that seemed to be brewing? Yet she realized that she had no choice. If battle came, she would join in.

The two groups stood staring at each other for a long moment. Then, to Cara's astonishment, three of the delvers carefully placed their spears on the ground. Holding their empty hands before them, they took ten steps into the clearing.

Cara edged closer to Lightfoot and laid her hand on his flank.

"What's happening?"

"I don't know. Just listen. I can't talk to you now, I have to pay attention to the enemy."

She made no response but kept her hand in place.

One of the delvers spoke. His voice was harsh, and the words Cara heard held no meaning at all. But through Lightfoot she understood the delver to be asking if they could talk rather than fight.

Lightfoot dipped his horn in response to the delver's request. The Dimblethum growled suspiciously. The Squijum seemed to have disappeared altogether.

Cara wondered how the unicorn would communicate with the delvers. Would he have to pierce their hearts, as he had her own? To her surprise, he was able to approximate their language with sounds made deep in his throat.

"What business do the Children of the Earth have

with Lightfoot, son of Dancing Heart, son of Arabella Skydancer?"

She blinked in surprise. Was Lightfoot the Queen's grandson?

"My name is Nedzik," replied the delver spokesman, his huge eyes shifting from side to side as if he was expecting trouble at any moment. "I come to you on business that is shameful, but necessary."

The other delvers muttered nervously.

"Go on," said Lightfoot.

"Though there is no love lost between unicorn and delver, we live in the same world — "

"Through treachery," growled the Dimblethum.

Lightfoot shot him a warning glance. The Dimblethum fell silent, though Cara could see it was an effort for him. Lightfoot turned back to the delver. "Go on," he said again.

Nedzik hesitated. He looked as if he was considering dropping the matter or simply fighting instead. The others shifted uneasily. Finally he spoke again.

"Though we live in the same world, many of my people hate the unicorns so violently that they would do anything to strike at them. They would do this even if such a blow might bring great damage, even destruction, to all of Luster." He paused, looked behind him to the others, then continued. "That is the way things stand now. That is why we have come to speak to you, though doing so means we are betraying our king."

He was blinking rapidly, and Cara realized that the sunlight hurt his enormous eyes.

"What does the Delverking plan?" asked Lightfoot. Though it was not in his words, Cara could sense the confusion and fear that the delver's message had created in him.

Nedzik took a step back and the other two weaponless delvers gathered around him. After a moment of whispering, he stepped forward again.

"The king wishes to open a door to the world of men so that they can enter Luster and hunt the unicorns."

The shock that ran through Lightfoot caused Cara to momentarily lift her hand from his flank. When she put it back, the delver was still speaking.

" . . . a thought long in his mind. But until now, he did not have a way to implement it. That changed when Gamzil came upon the human child that stands next to you and tore from her the amulet she was wearing."

The Dimblethum growled at the memory, causing the delver spokesman to flinch.

"Gamzil is a fool and did not recognize the amulet for what it is. He tried to steal it only because it is a pretty bauble. Not long after he came crying back to our caves without it, a man came to us, a human, who had just crossed here from Earth."

Cara caught her breath. The delver was almost certainly speaking of the man who had chased her and her grandmother into St. Christopher's. How had he made it through? Did he have an amulet of his own — or had he somehow managed to jump through the opening she had created? A wave of guilt washed through her, and she was glad that Lightfoot could not read her thoughts unless she sent them to him.

"This man began to ask questions," continued Nedzik, "and it was not long before King Gnurflax, who is smarter than he is wise, may the rocks not crush my feet, realized what he was seeking. When he also realized that Gamzil had had this very amulet in his hands and then lost it, his rage was mighty indeed." Nedzik shook his enormous head. "Alas, poor Gamzil. Even a fool does not deserve such a fate. Anyway, the king has sent out many groups in search of the child and the amulet. It was only luck that let us find you first."

The Dimblethum's growl grew deeper. The delvers looked profoundly embarrassed.

"What the king plans to do with the amulet has not been made widely known," continued the delver. "Those among us who do know his intentions are disturbed but for the most part willing to go along. My cousins and I think this is madness. We believe that flinging open the doors will mean death and destruction for all of us.

"Make no mistake: What we do now is treason. Should the king discover us, should word of this reach his ears, it will mean our lives. But so, we believe, will the success of his plan. He seeks the child and the amulet. You must flee, flee with all speed, flee with one eye before you and one eye watching behind. If you let the amulet fall into the hands of my people, the madness of our king will bring doom to us all."

He began to back away from them.

"Wait!" said Lightfoot.

Nedzik took another step back, then paused. "We must go. Every moment we talk with you rather than fight you we risk our lives."

"You have our gratitude," said Lightfoot, bowing his head. He hesitated, then said, "Will you travel with us? Should we meet others of your kind the battle may go against us. If you truly believe your king's plan will cause such disaster, help us avert it."

"That we cannot do," said Nedzik, and Cara could sense a note of regret in his words. "We have done more than we should as it is." He paused, then added, "We can do this much more. We will point the chase in another direction. That should give you some time. Use it wisely."

With that, the creatures faded into the forest so swiftly and completely it was as if they had never been there at all.

The Squijum came racing down a tree. "Nasty phooey strange hotcha no-good trustem?" he chattered, his lush gray tail twitching violently.

Lightfoot shook himself, a shudder that ran from his shoulders through his flank, and muttered, "This is enough to make me wish my uncle were here."

"What do you think we should do?" growled the Dimblethum.

"Head for Grimwold's Cavern as fast as we can. It's the closest safe haven. Besides, we may be able to get a message to the Queen from there."

"How?" asked Cara.

"Talk later!" cried the Squijum. "Now now shake butts move feet hotcha get going!"

"The Squijum is right," said Lightfoot. "The sooner we're away from this place the better. And we have at least a seven-day journey ahead of us."

"Not necessarily," said the Dimblethum. "There is a shorter way. . . ."

Lightfoot snorted. "Shorter, certainly — unless *she* catches us. In that case, we will never get there at all."

"She?" asked Cara nervously.

"Firethroat, Firethroat!" squeaked the Squijum. He began to run in circles around Lightfoot's hooves, crying, "Run run hide hide cover butts not safe hotcha!"

Lightfoot sighed. "Of Luster's seven dragons, Firethroat is the oldest and wisest. She is also the one least to be trifled with. She guards her territory well, does not take trespass lightly, and has no use for fools — a fact my uncle says would make it particularly dangerous for *me* to come in contact with her."

"The choice is simple," said the Dimblethum, backing up to a tree and rubbing his shoulders against it. "The Dimblethum and his friends take the long way and spend seven or eight days trying to avoid the delvers. Or they take the short route and spend a day and a half hoping Firethroat is not angered by them walking the edge of her territory." He pushed against the tree harder, sighed, then added, "The Dimblethum does not think the delvers will expect anyone to go that way. Even if they do, they will not follow unless King Gnurflax is more desperate than the Dimblethum thinks. So the Dimblethum says take the short route. If Firethroat is in a bad mood and eats the Dimblethum and his friends, at least the amulet is saved from the delvers."

For that there was no answer. So it was decided that they would take the dragonpath to Grimwold's Cavern.

"It's just as well, in a way," Lightfoot said to Cara later on. "It's a much prettier route, and you will see some amazing things. Still and all . . ."

He left the sentence unfinished. She could tell he was contemplating the fate of a fool in the claws of a dragon.

9

THE HUNTED

They set off through the forest and did not stop when darkness fell. Lightfoot, putting all his energy into finding the way — and avoiding detection — was distracted and unwilling to talk.

Cara began to stumble again. After a bit the Dimblethum picked her up and carried her in his arms. She fell asleep nestled against his warm and furry breast. When she woke, she gestured to him that she wanted to walk. He hesitated, then set her gently on her feet. She wished she could speak to him; she wanted to thank him for the ride.

By the nearly full moon that shone through the drooping trees she saw that they had entered a swamp. Ahead of her, the Squijum was riding on

Lightfoot's back as the unicorn picked his way along a trail that led between large stretches of brackish water.

Strange dark things fluttered through the night air above them. Occasionally one would swoop close to Cara, and the whir of its rapidly beating wings would give her a start. The first time this happened she cried out in fear, but after that she kept her silence — partly because the Dimblethum had laid a heavy paw on her shoulder and scowled at her, indicating that such outbursts were a bad idea.

So eager was she to please, to prove she was fit for this adventure, that when something snakelike slithered across their path she stopped short but managed to hold in her cry of fear. The serpent stared at her for a moment. Suddenly, without warning, it reared up and hissed at her, spreading a vivid red hood that actually glowed in the darkness. Then she did scream, and jump backward as well.

She bumped into the Dimblethum, who seemed as startled as she was, for he, too, let out a sound of surprise. Then, leaning over her, he roared at the serpent. The sound hurt Cara's ears. The serpent hissed again, more softly. The Dimblethum made a menacing growl deep in his throat. Cara's heart pounded, and her skin grew cold as she stared at the serpent, wondering whether it would strike at her. The Dimblethum continued his low growl until the serpent finally dropped to its belly. Slithering forward, it slipped silently into the murky water.

Cara didn't object when the Dimblethum picked her up and carried her again.

In this way, passing through swamp and field and forest, along the edges of low cliffs, beside swiftly running crystal streams, they arrived in two days at the edge of Firethroat's territory.

They had stopped to sleep twice, at which times Cara had been fed nuts and berries and a kind of root the Squijum dug up.

"What is it?" she had asked the first time he came scampering up with one of the dark brown roots in his paws and handed it to her.

"We call it *tarka*," replied Lightfoot, resting his horn on her shoulder. "Twist it and see what happens."

When she did as he directed, the root's nubbly husk popped open, revealing a crisp, white interior.

"Try it," said the unicorn.

To her surprise, it tasted like sweet almonds. "Good!" she said, smiling at the Squijum.

"Yah, yah hotcha like it," he replied, dashing off into the darkness. He returned a few minutes later with another of the roots. Stopping three or four feet in front of her, he chittered something she could not understand, then tossed her the root. She caught it before it landed in her lap, prompting an enthusiastic burst of chatter from the Squijum.

Acting on impulse, she picked up a nut and tossed it to him. Leaping into the air, the little creature caught the nut a foot and a half above the ground.

Then he bounded over to her, dropped the nut in her lap, and ran about twenty feet away.

"You like to play catch!" she cried in delight, tossing him the nut again.

The Squijum caught it handily, and Cara spent another fifteen minutes tossing him various objects she found on the forest floor. He caught almost all of them, missing only if her throws were absurdly wide of the mark. The leaps, twists, and turns he made in accomplishing these catches were so wild that she found herself laughing out loud, the first time she had done so in longer than she could remember.

Lightfoot and the Dimblethum took turns watching at night. Feeling safe in their care, Cara slept soundly. Yet she found herself tormented by strange dreams in which she was hunted by some faceless horror.

The second night she was woken from one of these dreams by the Dimblethum, who placed a huge paw gently over her mouth to keep her from crying out. After a moment, when he was sure she was awake and calm, he uncovered her mouth.

Soon after, Lightfoot came to her. His horn looked as if it had been carved from the bright and shining moon. Placing it across her shoulder, he said, "We're being trailed."

Fighting down her fear, she replied, "How do you know?"

"The Squijum was out hunting and spotted a camp. We need to move ahead as fast as possible while its owner is still resting."

Cara furrowed her brow. "Just one of them? I thought the delvers would be hunting us in packs."

"It's not a delver," replied Lightfoot. "It's the man."

Fully awake now, she rose quickly, silently, and followed Lightfoot out of their camp. The Dimblethum lagged behind. When she turned to look back, she saw him moving about the spot, trying to erase all signs that they had been there.

The Squijum was nowhere to be seen.

Digging her hand in her pocket to make sure the amulet was in its place, she trudged on through the darkness.

So obsessed were they with the danger behind that they did not remember Nedzik's warning to flee with one eye watching before them.

Thus it was that they did not see the delver camp until they had nearly stumbled into it.

Lightfoot stopped so abruptly that Cara bumped into him. Only the effort she had spent training herself not to cry out when they were traveling through the swamp kept her from betraying their presence with a shout.

Moving cautiously up beside Lightfoot, she froze when she saw not far ahead a low fire, little more than a bed of glowing coals. It was surrounded by dark forms that she took to be sleeping delvers. The reason she assumed they were delvers was that the two figures keeping watch by the fire most definitely were.

More than ever, she was glad of the ability to communicate with Lightfoot without speaking. "What do we do now?" she asked.

"I believe a quiet retreat is in order," he replied silently, beginning to back away.

Cara had long ago noticed the unicorn's ability to move through the forest without making a single sound. She, alas, possessed no such skill. Despite her best efforts, she stepped on a dry twig that broke beneath her foot. It was a tiny sound, yet in the silence of the forest it exploded against her horrified ears like a firecracker.

Lightfoot froze where he stood. She did the same until the delver guards leaped to their feet and, with a bloodcurdling scream, started after them.

"On my back!" ordered Lightfoot.

She obeyed without hesitation. No sooner had she scrambled onto his shoulders than he was off like a rocket, hurtling into the darkness. Hunched low over his shoulders, Cara wrapped her hands in his silky mane and prayed that she would be able to hold on. Branches whipped against her as they careened wildly through the forest. Dark shapes rose before them, then vanished to the side as Lightfoot veered around them.

So tightly were Cara and Lightfoot connected that for a moment she felt as if she *were* the unicorn, as if it were her legs doing the running, her aching lungs and hammering heart fueling the flight from the delvers.

They plunged through a misty hollow, up a steep bank, in and out of patches of moonlight, until suddenly Lightfoot stopped, flanks heaving, and stood silent, listening.

In the distance they could hear delvers crying out in anger and frustration.

"We've lost them," he said triumphantly.

It was only then that Cara realized how terrified she had been. Trying to stop the trembling that suddenly overtook her, she said, "You must be able to see in the dark. I had no idea where we were going."

"Half the time, neither did I," confessed the unicorn.

Cara caught her breath in surprise, then started to laugh.

Their moment of triumph was short-lived. From the dark and the distance they heard a terrible roar, followed by angry battle cries. The sounds were confusing, jumbled together, and muted by distance. But when silence fell, there was no question what they meant.

"They've got the Dimblethum," whispered Cara in horror.

10

THE TINKER

ara and Lightfoot stood about a hundred feet from the delver camp. They had debated fiercely about who should go back to study the situation. When Lightfoot claimed he could move more silently, Cara pointed out that he was also more likely to be seen because of his white coat and luminous horn.

"Actually, I can dim the horn," he told her. "It would be a dangerous thing if I couldn't."

"That doesn't change the fact that it's a lot easier to see that white coat of yours than it would be to spot me. I mean look at me — I practically blend into the forest!"

Indeed, her jeans and T-shirt were so stained and

mud spattered that they looked like the camouflage clothes the boys in her class sometimes wore.

"I can't let you go down there alone," said Lightfoot firmly. "If they heard you, how would you get away?"

In the end they decided they would go together, but Cara would make the closest approach to the camp, with Lightfoot hiding nearby. She agreed solemnly not to get more than fifty feet away from him.

They also decided that it would be foolish to take the amulet with them.

"You know, not all my relatives would approach this the same way," said Lightfoot, resting his horn on Cara's shoulder as she carefully hid the amulet and its broken chain in a hollow tree. "I can think of some that would insist we abandon the Dimblethum and head for Grimwold's Cavern as fast as possible."

She thought about that for a minute. "It might be the sensible thing to do," she said. "After all, the most important thing is to keep the amulet from falling into the wrong hands."

"That's true," said Lightfoot.

Cara paused, her hand still in the tree trunk. "But leaving the Dimblethum doesn't feel right," she continued.

"That's true as well."

She could feel confusion beginning to creep over her. "So the question is, should we risk the mission, and the safety of *all* the unicorns, in order to rescue one friend?"

"Some of my relatives would say there is no question. We have a clear duty to keep the amulet away from the enemy. This is not just *our* journey. The safety of the unicorns, and possibly all of Luster, depends on defending the amulet against those who would abuse it."

Cara slowly drew her hand from the tree. She began moving her arm back and forth, as if she were trying to decide whether to reach in and take back the amulet. The choice seemed to be crushing against her brain. "Are you trying to tell me we shouldn't go back for the Dimblethum?" she asked.

"I'm just pointing out the questions involved. I should probably also point out that most of my relatives don't think much of the Dimblethum." He paused, then added, "Of course, most of them don't think much of me, either."

Though she longed for Lightfoot to make the decision, Cara sensed that he was going to defer to her in this matter — perhaps because he was confused himself. But she was torn, too. Her mind was telling her that for the good of all they should flee with the amulet, taking it as far from this place as possible. Her heart was screaming that they could not leave their friend.

In the end, her heart made the choice. Asking herself what her grandmother would do, she found herself thinking instead about her parents. The painful memory of the way they had abandoned her made it impossible for her to do the same to anyone else.

"We're going to get him," she declared.

"That's a very immature decision," said Lightfoot.

The criticism stung like a slap. "Why do you say that?" she asked sharply.

"Because it is what I would choose," he replied, sounding amused. "And my uncle has assured me many times that I am very immature."

"If your uncle wants to handle this, let him come out here and wander around in the woods with the delvers," said Cara. "In the meantime, we have to go see what they're doing with the Dimblethum."

Creeping through the darkness, away from Lightfoot and toward the delvers, Cara could easily have wished they had decided to press on in their journey. Each movement was an agony of indecision as she tried not to make a betraying sound. Each dew-wet leaf that brushed her face, each twig that prodded her side, seemed to her racing imagination the touch of an enemy.

Finally she drew close enough to get a clear view of the delver camp through the undergrowth. By the flickering light of the low fire she saw that the Dimblethum had been bound to a tall pole. He sagged against his ropes, as if weary and beaten. Even in the low light she could see at least two hideous wounds.

The delvers stood in a circle around him, prodding him with their spears. They were speaking to him, but without Lightfoot at her side, she heard only rasping, guttural sounds. The Dimblethum spoke not at all; whether he was refusing to answer or had actually lost consciousness she could not tell in the dim light.

Each time one of the delvers poked at the manbear she wanted to scream at them to leave him alone. Finally she could stand to watch no more. Moving quietly, she returned to Lightfoot's side.

"What can we do?" she asked after describing the hideous scene.

He shook his head mournfully. "I do not know."

They trailed the delvers for the better part of the next day. It was a horrible, frustrating time, partly because they were moving backward, away from Grimwold's Cavern, but even more because in that time they were not able to do anything to help the Dimblethum.

To add to their worries, they had no idea what had happened to the man who was hunting Cara. She couldn't help but wonder if he was stalking them even as they were following the delvers.

To top things off, the Squijum — who would normally have reappeared by this time — seemed to have vanished altogether.

"You don't suppose anything happened to him, do you?" asked Cara once when they were taking a break.

"Hard to tell with that one," replied Lightfoot.

74

"Something *could* have happened to him. Or he may simply have lost track of us — though he is a very good hunter. He may even have lost interest; his attention span is not all that great. But there is nothing we can do about him now. We need to focus on the Dimblethum. I'd suggest you rest while you can. There's no telling when they'll start moving again."

Though she couldn't stop worrying, Cara did try to relax. They were only taking a break because the delvers had stopped for the same purpose. There were an even dozen of the little monsters, about half the group that had first captured the Dimblethum. According to the snatches of conversation they had been able to catch, the others had remained to continue looking for "the girl with the amulet," as they referred to her.

Cara thought it was rather amusing that while they were out looking for her she was trailing them. It was the only amusing aspect of the situation. Her heart ached for the poor Dimblethum. She had caught glimpses of him stumbling along, his paws bound behind him, delvers prodding him with their spears should he falter or slow. Oddly, the delvers seemed not to worry about anyone coming after them. She decided that they were so used to being the hunters that it never occurred to them that things might go the other way.

The delver party got ready to start out again. It was a noisy process, which made it easy for Cara and

Lightfoot to keep track of them without getting too close. Cara had noticed that while the delvers occasionally moved through unmarked forest, they more often followed faint but definite paths. What surprised her was that twice these paths crossed wider paths defined by pairs of shallow ruts.

"Is this some kind of road?" she asked Lightfoot the first time they crossed one.

"Yes. It was made by some of the humans."

"There are other humans in Luster?" she asked excitedly.

"Not many."

She wanted to know more, but he was focused on the problem of the delvers and the Dimblethum and didn't want to be bothered talking about such things. She did notice that though the delvers crossed these roads, they did not follow them.

She and Lightfoot were crossing one of the roads themselves, some minutes behind the delvers, when they heard a horrible clatter to their right.

"There you are!" cried a friendly voice. "I've been waiting for you!"

They turned. To their astonishment an oddly dressed man was trotting toward them. He was drawing a cart behind him, which he pulled by means of two wooden poles. Hanging from the roof of the cart were all manner of things, including a number of pots and pans, all of them clanging and clattering like a cooking set being rolled down a stairway.

Cara was terrified that the racket would draw the

delvers, but Lightfoot told her that it was more likely they would stay away, since they did not care much for humans, and only humans would make such a racket.

Still, she would have insisted that they move on, so that they not lose sight of the Dimblethum, had she not seen what was sitting on top of the man's wagon.

"The Squijum!" she cried.

"Oh, yes," said the man, slowing to a walk. "It was he who brought me to you."

"Good Squijum! Happy good hotcha-gotcha!" cried the little creature, leaping from the wagon to an overhanging tree. He began swinging through the branches, which let him reach Cara and Lightfoot considerably ahead of the man. He leaped down to her shoulder.

Cara stroked his fur as she stared at the approaching man.

Bald and bearded, with a roundish nose, he wore high leather boots, loose trousers, and a remarkable coat that seemed to be made almost entirely of patches of various bright fabrics. The coat had an astonishing number of pockets. Gold chains drooped in graceful arcs from every one of them.

"Thank goodness I found you," he said, clattering to a stop. Dropping the wooden poles of his wagon, he wiped his high bald head with a handkerchief he fished from his trousers.

The cart was like a tiny house on wheels, about

four feet wide and eight feet long. It had a pitched roof, and high blue walls. Painted on its side in large, old-fashioned letters, were the words:

THOMAS THE TINKER
I Mend What I Can

"Actually, you're right on schedule," he said, pulling one of the chains to reveal a large pocket watch. He stared at the watch for a moment, then frowned. "Or maybe you're not." He pulled an even larger watch from another pocket and stared at it. "Oh, well, never mind," he said, shoving both watches back into pockets other than the ones from which they had come. "You're here, and so am I, and that's what matters. Shall we take a stab at rescuing your friend?"

11

THE CART

hree hours later, Cara crouched in the narrow aisle that ran down the center of the Tinker's wagon. The Squijum sat next to her, nearly bursting with the effort of keeping still. With Thomas hauling the cart, they were heading for the delvers' camp.

Cara was surprised at how smoothly the cart traveled. She had expected to be bounced and jolted for the entire journey.

The inside of the cart had also surprised her. Rather than the hopelessly cluttered jumble she had anticipated it was so tidy as to be almost stark. Whatever Thomas carried here was packed behind rows and rows of small doors, tiny ones at the top of the cart, larger ones at the bottom.

Despite the need to remain silent, she had tried to open a few of the little doors. When they had proved to be locked, she had tried the others. Every one of them (dozens in all, counting the smallest) was locked.

It had been very frustrating.

In her hand she held the knife Thomas had given her. "When the time comes, I want you to jump out of the wagon," he had told her. "Cut the Dimblethum free and guide him back inside. Then close the door — quickly and *tightly!* — and I'll get you out of there."

The whole thing had been set up so fast it had left her head spinning. But that was the first thing she had noticed about the Tinker: He was fast. It didn't make any difference what he was doing — walking, talking, thinking, or planning — he did it rapidly. Lightfoot had seemed alternately amused and disgusted by the man, but since they had no other way of saving the Dimblethum, he had had little choice but to accept the assistance.

Cara wished she were able to talk to the Squijum. She wanted to know more details about how he had found the Tinker.

Suddenly the cart stopped. Moving silently, she pressed her eye to the secret hole Thomas had showed her in the back wall. It took a moment for her to make out the scene. It was fully dark now, and they were in the delvers' camp, which was once again lit by a low fire. The creatures, none of them any higher than Thomas's waist, had gathered around the Tinker. Several were shifting their spears in a menacing fashion.

Thomas spoke to them rapidly in their own language. His hands flying, he pointed first to their spears, then to the cart.

For a terrifying moment, Cara wondered if he had betrayed them and was sending the delvers to kill her.

She beat down her suspicions and tried to spot the Dimblethum. But the limited view offered by the peephole made it impossible to see him. She hoped she would be able to find him fast enough when the time came!

As she watched, one of the delvers reluctantly handed Thomas his spear. The Tinker took something from his pouch and made a series of swift strokes over the spearhead. Then he tested it against his thumb, and with a smile handed it back to the delver, who did the same thing. His hideous face broke into a wide grin and he nodded to the others.

Wonderful, Thomas, thought Cara. *Sharpen their weapons for them. That's going to do us a lot of good!*

But he only sharpened two more of the weapons. When he took the third he examined it and made a series of clucking noises that indicated big trouble. Turning to the owner he said something to him, then reached into one of his pockets and drew out a watch.

Cara braced herself. That was the sign.

But when Thomas opened the watch, nothing happened. He shook it in disgust, closed it, put it back in his pocket. Then he dug out another one.

He motioned to the delvers and they gathered closer.

Thomas opened the watch and, even though she had been expecting it, Cara cried out at the flash of blinding white light that filled the clearing. Her cry, however, was nothing compared to the screams of the delvers, who clamped their hands over their enormous eyes and fell to the ground screaming in pain.

Cara shot out of the cart. After the flash of light, the clearing seemed extraordinarily dark, and it took her a second to spot the Dimblethum. As the night before, he was tied to a pole. Racing to his side, she slashed the rough cords that held him.

The look of gratitude on his face made the risk and the effort all worthwhile. He stumbled forward and she feared that he would not be able to walk. If that happened she didn't know what she would do, for she surely could not carry him.

He did not fall, but he did need to lean on her shoulder. Staggering under his weight, she guided him back to the cart. Chaos surrounded them as the still-blinded delvers, most of them not yet back on their feet, groped their way about the clearing, screaming and cursing. She could not understand any of the words except Thomas's name, which they screamed over and over in tones that made her blood run cold.

One delver nearly stumbled into them, but the Squijum leaped at him from behind, causing him to spin and fall to his knees. Hurrying past him, Cara led the Dimblethum into the cart, turning him sideways so that his broad shoulders could fit into the narrow aisle that ran down the center.

The Squijum leaped in behind her. Slamming the door shut, she fastened the bolt and prayed.

Thomas was as good as his word. With her eye pressed to the peephole, Cara could see the trees flashing by as he pulled them through the forest to the place where they were supposed to rendezvous with Lightfoot. This time she decided that there must be something magical about the cart, for no one could pull it over the root-ribbed forest floor so swiftly and easily without magic.

Lightfoot was waiting impatiently in a clearing just off the side of the little road, about two miles from the delver camp. He had wanted to come on the mission, but the others had persuaded him that there had to be at least one of them left should things come to disaster, and he was the logical one to stay behind.

"From what you've told me, we'll need you to heal the Dimblethum when we get him back," Thomas had said. He had paused, then added (not without a note of jealousy), "I wish I could do *that* kind of mending. Anyway, no sense in risking you at this stage of the game."

Lightfoot had fussed and fumed but agreed to stay behind, muttering that there were times when he found it utterly annoying that he did not have hands. However, once they pulled the Dimblethum out of the cart, he was in his glory. Making the others step aside, he used his horn to heal the numerous wounds that split the manbear's pelt.

Cara noticed with some surprise that the horn glowed brighter as it was doing the healing. What did not surprise her was that as soon as Lightfoot was done, his knees buckled and he fell to the ground.

"We need to get farther away from here," said Thomas nervously. "Let's get them into the wagon."

"They'll never fit!" said Cara.

"Oh, ye of little faith," laughed Thomas. "Watch this."

Though she watched, Cara was never really sure just what it was that the Tinker did to the cart. He began pulling out rods and folding down slats. Humming to himself as he worked, he reminded her of nothing so much as a kid playing with one of those toys that, with the right motions, can be turned into something altogether different. And indeed, when Thomas was done, the blue cart was twice the size it had been.

"How did you do that?" she asked in astonishment

as the Squijum raced around the cart, chattering with excitement.

"This is a very special wagon," said Thomas with a chuckle.

How special became even clearer when he offered to let Cara pull it, after they had loaded the Dimblethum and Lightfoot inside.

"You're joking!" she said, looking at the cart, which was now the size of a large camper trailer.

"Give it a try," he replied gleefully.

Stationing herself between the poles, she grabbed them firmly and tried to take a step forward.

The cart rolled easily behind her.

"Very special indeed," he said, giving the cart an approving pat.

The only problem with having the cart so large was it would not pass easily through the forest. They were forced to follow the road instead, though Thomas said that was just as well, since the delvers would tend to avoid it.

"They won't be able to see well enough to follow us for another few hours, anyway," he continued. "Then they'll probably have a long fight about whether they *should* follow us, or report back to the king, or just run away and hide for a month or two. So the odds are we won't need to worry about them for a while."

"There's someone else hunting for us," said Cara nervously. "Another human."

"I know," said Thomas with a nod. "The Squijum and I met him on the road. Unfortunately, I was a little confused at the time. I'm afraid I completely bollixed the directions I gave him. In fact, now that I think of it, I probably sent him the wrong way altogether. I expect he's a long way away from us now." He gave her a wink. "Silly of me," he said, "but it's done now. Oh, well — I was pretty sure he was no friend of the Queen's."

Cara smiled. Much as she had come to love Lightfoot, the Dimblethum, and the Squijum, they were all very different from her. Thomas's presence made her realize that she had missed human company more than she would have thought possible.

"How did *you* get here?" she asked him now as he strolled along beside her.

"Fell in by accident," he said. "Pretty silly of me, now that I think about it. But then, I've done a lot of silly things in my time."

"How long ago did it happen?"

"Oh, it's hard to say." He stopped and did some calculations on his fingers. "About a hundred and fifty years ago, give or take five years on either side."

"Right," she sneered. "And I'll be ninety-two on my next birthday."

He chuckled, which he seemed to do fairly often. "Such a cynic for one so young. I have drunk from the Queen's Pool — a reward for a little something I did when I first got here. Won't make me live forever, which is a pretty frightening idea, anyway now that I think of it. But it does stretch things out a bit."

She looked at him, wondering if he was teasing her. The thing was, here in Luster such an outlandish statement made almost perfect sense.

"Ah, here we go," he said before she could ask another question. "This looks to me like a good place to bed down for the night. And just in time, too," he added, holding out his hand at the same time that Cara felt the first drops of rain begin to spatter against her forearms.

At Thomas's direction, she positioned the cart about ten feet off the road. Rushing about with his usual speed, he quickly blocked up the wheels, folded out a side compartment complete with a bed, unrolled a canopy from the back, and started a small fire in its shelter.

"There we go," he said, settling on the steps that he had flipped out from under the back of the cart. "Cozy as a house and twice as easy to pick up and move."

Cara went in the back of the cart to check on Lightfoot and the Dimblethum, but both of them were sleeping soundly. The Squijum, which had scurried in behind her, snuck onto the Dimblethum's stomach. Covering his eyes with his tail, he sighed softly and fell asleep.

"Now I know this cart is magical," muttered Cara, climbing back down to sit beside the Tinker.

12

DRAGONPATH TO GRIMWOLD

The next morning Lightfoot and the Dimblethum were still a little shaky. However, they
both pronounced themselves fit to travel.

"Mind if I come along?" asked the Tinker,
as he started to fold up his cart. To Cara's
astonishment, he continued folding until it was about
the size of a man's wallet.

"Convenient sort of a thing, isn't it?" he said with
a smile, slipping the cart into his pocket. "Only real
problem I have with it is when I want to get at my
tools. Then I have to unfold the silly thing all over
again."

The Dimblethum came to her while she was standing with Lightfoot, and said, "For what you did, the

Dimblethum thanks you. Now the Dimblethum and you are even, each rescuing the other."

Cara was startled. "I didn't come get you so we would be even," she said, somewhat sharply. "I did it because . . . oh, never mind."

Lightfoot translated her words for the Dimblethum, who looked truly puzzled, and a little hurt. But later he gave Cara a flower, one of the fuzzy purple ones. She tucked it over her ear and wore it for the rest of the day.

Most of this day was given over to retrieving the amulet. They had to retrace their journey of the day before, and it was late afternoon when they finally reached the area where Cara had hidden it. For a little while they were not able to find the specific tree. Cara was beginning to panic when the Squijum located it, working by scent.

"See, see!" he cried triumphantly. "*Can* look and find!" Emerging from the hollow tree with the amulet and its broken chain, he crooned to himself, "Hotcha good finder guy!"

That accomplished, they needed to plan what to do next.

"If we press on, we can reach the edge of Dragon Territory tonight," said Thomas. "That will give us an extra bit of safety if the delvers are still patrolling the area; it is unlikely they will enter Firethroat's domain."

"Which makes them smarter than us," muttered Lightfoot.

*   *   *

Late in the evening they stopped to rest. The Dimblethum built a small fire while Thomas unfolded his cart. Later, after they had eaten, he asked Cara if she would let him examine the amulet.

"Well, now I see what the fuss is all about," he said, as he turned it over and over in his hands. "It's not every day that one of the Queen's Five turns up out in the open. Would you like me to fix this silly chain?" he asked.

"That would be nice," said Cara.

"I like fixing things," he said as he worked. "The world is always breaking, here and there, this way and that. Fix a bit of it, and I feel like I'm helping."

Reaching into his jacket, he pulled out a ridiculously tiny tool.

"Funny thing about chains," he said. "They're everywhere, once you know how to look for them. I like chains."

When Cara laughed at this, he shook his chest, causing the hundreds of golden links that hung there to sparkle in the firelight.

"There's lots of kinds of chains," he continued. "You can't see most of them, the ones that bind folks together. But people build them, link by link. Sometimes the links are weak, snap like this one did. That's another funny thing, now that I think of it. Sometimes when you mend a chain, the place where you fix it is strongest of all."

As he spoke, he held up the chain, which was whole again. Passing the amulet to Cara, he said, "Never was a chain that couldn't be broken. Sometimes it's even a good idea."

Putting away his tools, he crawled under the wagon and slept.

Despite her worries about her grandmother, Cara found herself beginning to fall deeply in love with the world into which she had fallen.

"It's so lovely here," she marveled as they stood on top of a high hill, gazing over a spread of green territory dotted with small lakes, friendly rivers, and patches of forest.

"Earth used to be like this," replied Lightfoot. "Not all green, of course; it always had its mountains and deserts. Luster does, too, for that matter. But Earth was once clean and bright and beautiful."

"How do you know about that?" she asked.

"It's in our stories. It's where we came from, after all. Grimwold can tell you more."

"Who is this Grimwold, anyway?"

"A friend of the unicorns," said Lightfoot. "He came here long ago and stayed, as friends sometimes do. More than that I had best not say. He is very possessive and does not like others to tell his stories."

"Is he human?"

"Close enough. Scratch right there, please."

She obliged, scratching his shoulder where she had been resting her hand. She was about to ask him about Summerhaven when he whispered, "Look!"

To their left stood a range of snowcapped mountains. Cara had been eyeing it nervously as they traveled and had been relieved when her companions had assured her that they were not going to have to cross it. Now she looked at it again, wondering what Lightfoot wanted her to see.

Suddenly she caught her breath. Far away, soaring above the highest of the peaks, was the form of a dragon. It was tiny to the eye, but given its distance from them, she could tell it must be enormous.

"Firethroat?" she asked without opening her mouth.

"None other," replied the unicorn.

Even the Squijum was quiet as they watched the great creature swoop and soar above the mountains. Suddenly she turned and sailed in their direction. Cara felt her heart leap in a strange combination of wonder and fear as the dragon opened her mouth and shot forth a column of flame nearly as long as she was herself.

"She's beautiful!" thought Cara, even as she wondered if they were about to die. Then, to Lightfoot: "Should we run?"

"No! If she hasn't seen us — which is unlikely — it will only attract her. If she has, it will anger her, make her think we are up to no good. Our best choice is to stand still and hope she is in a quiet mood."

The dragon continued to spiral and weave through the air. As she drew closer, Cara could see that she was red, a deep red, like blood and fire. Just when Cara thought that she couldn't hold still for another moment, the dragon banked to the left, flapped her wings, and — moving faster than Cara would have thought possible — returned to the mountain. A moment later she had vanished.

"Yowee hotcha yipes!" squeaked the Squijum, vaulting onto Lightfoot's back. "Big eater make me supper gone gone good yipe now!"

Cara laughed in spite of herself. "Since she didn't attack, do you think she approves of us?"

"I wouldn't go so far as to say that," replied Lightfoot. "Just that she doesn't disapprove. Madame Firethroat does not dislike unicorns. It is uninvited company she disapproves of. I suspect she found our little group odd enough that she would rather watch us than eat us. Likely she guesses that we're heading for Grimwold's Cavern. As long as we don't do anything to annoy her, I think she'll let us alone."

"What would annoy her?" asked Cara nervously.

"Hunting on her territory, mostly," said Thomas. "She guards it jealously and considers anything that lives here to be hers. That, and anything that might hurt the land. She has no use for delvers, of course, with all their digging and changing things."

Lightfoot translated the comment for the Dimblethum, who replied, "No one has much use for delvers, except delvers. The Dimblethum and his friends should move on. They may have passed inspection, but Lady Firethroat has been known to change her mind. They should not press her tolerance."

They picked their way down the hillside, which was rocky but easy to walk on. Lower down, the waving grass was as high as Cara's waist, and Lightfoot invited her to ride on his back. The grassland was rife with flowers that grew on spikes so tall she could pluck them simply by stretching out her hand. She started weaving them into Lightfoot's mane until he shook his head and told her to stop.

Sometimes the Squijum rode on the Dimblethum's shoulders, sometimes with Cara. Sometimes he simply scampered off through the grass. Once he disappeared for a long, silent time. Cara started to worry, but finally he reappeared, smiling to himself.

"Don't do that again!" said Lightfoot harshly.

"Hungry small quiet! Not good not eat! Feed good!" protested the Squijum. But his voice was quiet, and he sounded abashed, even ashamed.

"Nothing that happens here is too small for Firethroat to notice," replied Lightfoot. "*Nothing*. Take a meal and you may make a meal, if you know what I mean."

The Squijum sulked and did not talk for several hours, while Cara scanned the sky nervously, wondering if Firethroat would now return for them. She continued to scan the sky as it grew dark, and myriads of twinkling stars began to appear above her. Their strange patterns and unusual brightness made her feel farther from home than ever.

They slept that night in the shelter of a low cliff. When the sun woke them they continued their journey. After the first hour, they veered to the right.

"We're leaving Firethroat's territory," said Lightfoot, and Cara felt both relief and regret to be turning away from the mighty dragon.

The region they traveled through now was one of high hills and rocky valleys. Late in the day they picked their way down the side of a hill to a valley through which ran a particularly lively stream. Halfway along the valley they started up the side of the hill again. After a moment, Cara realized that they were following a path. It led to a wooden door, set in the side of the hill.

"Grimwold's Cavern," said Lightfoot.

The Dimblethum stepped forward and banged on the door.

"Are you sure it's safe?" asked Cara nervously.

"Of course it's safe," said Lightfoot. "It's Grimwold's job to be here when we want to talk to him."

"His job?"

"I told you, he's the Keeper of the Chronicles. That's how he earns the right to be here. Anyone who wants to stay in Luster — "

His words were interrupted by the door swinging open. "All right, all right," said a gruff voice. "I hear you! What is it you want?"

Cara took one look at the strange little man standing before her and cried out in astonishment, "It's you!"

13

GRIMWOLD

"Who did you think it would be?" replied the little man sharply. "My cousin Droopwillow? He doesn't live here. Never did." He paused, then added, "Don't think he lives anywhere now, for that matter."

"But I've seen you before," Cara stammered, too surprised to notice that he was speaking to her in English. She stared at him to be sure that it was true. Yes, it had to be. The dark brown skin; the huge eyes, just this side of being so big they were grotesque; the thick, bushy brows that sprouted over them like silver waterfalls; the rounded pug nose — they all added up to the face she had seen every day on her grandmother's dresser.

Of course, there it had been surrounded by an ornate wooden frame. The image had not been a photograph like all the others on the dresser, but a painting, one her grandmother had done herself.

Whenever Cara had asked about the painting, Grandmother Morris had laughed and said, "Oh, *him*! an old friend from a long time ago — another life, almost. I painted that back when I was about fourteen."

Cara blinked at the memory. If her grandmother's words were true, then the little man standing in front of her had been a little *old* man for at least fifty years.

Lowering his extravagant eyebrows, Grimwold stared at her and said, "What do you mean, you've seen me before?"

"I . . . I think my grandmother must have met you. She has a picture of you on her dresser."

Grimwold smiled. "The ladies always did fancy me. What did you say your name was?"

"Cara. And how can you understand me without Lightfoot telling you what I'm saying?"

"It's my job. I take it you're Lightfoot," he added, turning to the unicorn. "Son of Dancing Heart, if I remember correctly, which I'm certain I do. Still breaking your mother's heart?"

Lightfoot blew air through his nostrils in a sign of anger. "We come seeking shelter and information. We also need to contact the Queen, if at all possible."

"Certainly, delighted, wonderful," grumbled the dwarf. "As if I don't have enough sorting and filing and figuring without you starting a new story on me. Well, come in, come in; you're outside now, and we're not going to get anywhere with you standing on the doorstep. I suppose the other three have to come in as well. I don't have their stories, you know, or at least not much of them. Not in the job, not in the job. Enough to do without keeping track of the likes of them."

The Squijum chittered angrily, but Cara had taken her hand from Lightfoot's shoulder, so she couldn't make out his words.

The door was wide enough for Cara and Lightfoot to enter side by side. The Squijum scampered in with them, racing around Lightfoot's cloven hooves. The Dimblethum lumbered through behind them. Thomas came last. Grimwold stood by the door until they were all inside. Then he slammed it shut and lowered a huge wooden crossbar to secure it.

They had entered a long tunnel. It was lit by softly glowing lanterns. To Cara's surprise, the walls were of wood rather than stone — a rich, dark wood that reminded her of the paneling in the old library where she and her grandmother had spent the after-noon that had ended with them being chased into St. Christopher's. How long ago had that been? She had lost count of the days.

Again she felt a stab of worry about her grandmother.

Mounted between the lanterns were beautiful paintings in intricately carved frames. Most of the images were of breathtaking landscapes populated by unicorns. Sometimes the unicorns were galloping, sometimes rearing and pawing the air, sometimes simply gazing out over their world. The remaining pictures were portraits, mostly of unicorns. Cara was amazed at how their faces varied, so that each displayed a distinct personality.

A handful of the portraits were of humans, or near-humans, since one was of a mermaid and another of a centaur. Cara wanted to stop to study the paintings, but Grimwold was hurrying them down the stone-paved hall. She was scurrying along, trying to keep up, when suddenly she did stop, so abruptly that the Dimblethum bumped into her.

"What is it?" asked Lightfoot, coming back and resting his horn on her shoulder.

Cara pointed to a small portrait of a beautiful red-haired girl in her early teens. "That's my grandmother!" she said, accidentally speaking aloud.

"It is?" asked Grimwold, sounding nearly as surprised as Cara. "Why didn't you tell me so in the first place? How is dear Ivy?"

"I don't know," said Cara desperately. "She was in terrible trouble when I left her."

Grimwold didn't look surprised. "I knew there was a tale in all this," he said. "Well, come along. We had best get on to the Story Room. I'm going to have to make notes. From the sound of it, I'm going to be part of this one, at least in a small way. Earth and sky, but I hate it when that happens."

Cara could have sworn she heard the Dimblethum chuckle. She glanced at him. His mouth was set in a straight line. Even so, he could not hide the twinkle in his eyes. She wished she knew what he was thinking!

The wood-paneled hall opened into a high cavern where the light came not from lanterns but from a single stone basin as wide as Cara was tall. Multi-colored flames leaped from its center, sending shadows flickering and dancing across the walls. The path wound between stalagmites that thrust upward from the floor and stalactites that hung down like huge stone fangs. A few pairs of stalactites and stalagmites had met, fusing into stone columns. Their smoothly shifting contours made them look as though muscles rippled beneath their slick surfaces.

The cavern was so large the bowl of fire could not clearly light its perimeter. Even so, the shifting flames revealed numerous doors and tunnel openings.

I wonder if you can get lost in here? thought Cara as Grimwold led them past the bowl of fire. To her surprise, it was cool — a witchfire that cast light only. She noticed then that it was smokeless as well.

Beyond the stone basin ran a stream about ten feet wide. Reflections of the firelight danced on the surface of the dark water. The stream was easily crossed by means of a number of wide, flat stepping stones. The Squijum bounded over ahead of them, then came leaping back. An angry gesture from the Dimblethum sent him scampering away again. Cara guessed that the manbear wanted no interference while trying to cross the stones.

Another wooden door, another wood-paneled corridor; this time the walls were broken on one side by doors, on the other by wood-framed openings that stretched into the darkness. The passage ended at a large door carved with strange designs. When Cara put her hand on Lightfoot's shoulder, she realized they said, "Story Room." It took her another moment to realize that if she could read them while in contact with Lightfoot, he must be able to read them as well.

"Let's get to work," said Grimwold.

Swinging wide the door, he invited them into what was, without doubt, the most wonderful room Cara had ever seen.

14

THE STORY ROOM

It was clearly a room made for writing. Books, scrolls, stacks of paper, notebooks, pens, and pots of ink seemed to cover every available surface — of which there were many, since the room held five long, low tables. The dark wooden walls were lined with maps, pictures, and intricately woven tapestries. Unlike the portraits in the first hall, these pictures seemed to illustrate specific events.

The walls (of which there were also many, for the room was full of nooks and crannies) were made of stone and wood. Natural outthrusts of stone had been carved into seats; some were even padded with cushions. Three of the larger indentations in the cavern walls had been transformed into lantern-lit reading nooks featuring shelves carved right into the stone. The shelves held pens, papers, and some little wooden figures.

In one wall a merry fire blazed in a huge fireplace. Unlike the cavern's witchfire, this one cast a lovely warmth. A broad shallow pit carved in front of the hearth provided a spot to sit and gaze into the flames.

It took Cara a moment to realize that the chairs were of many sizes. She suddenly suspected that the rugs scattered about the floor were, in fact, resting places for guests.

To the left of the fireplace a little stream sprang from an opening about five feet above the floor, creating a tiny waterfall. At its base was a pool about three feet in diameter. No stream ran out of the pool, so Cara assumed the water must somehow drain from the bottom.

Next to the little fall stood a rack that held a collection of cups and noggins of many sizes and shapes.

I want to live here! thought Cara.

"Find a place and settle in," said Grimwold as he scurried behind one of the tables. Mounting a stool, he spread a piece of curling paper before him, then set a polished rock at each corner to hold it down. Muttering to himself, he began trying to select a pen.

Lightfoot folded his legs and curled up on a deep purple rug. The Dimblethum and Thomas each picked up a wooden chair and moved it closer to the fire. After running about for a moment, the Squijum finally leaped into Thomas's lap; wrapping his tail around himself, he settled down with a sigh. (Three minutes later, however, he was climbing onto shelves and examining things.)

Cara hesitated, then positioned herself beside Lightfoot. Though she had wanted to sit with him all along, she had been afraid he would think she was clinging to him. Then she realized that if she didn't sit with him, she would not be able to understand anything the Dimblethum or the Squijum said.

"All right, what's your story?" asked Grimwold, looking directly at Cara.

"I beg your pardon?"

"Your story, your story," he said impatiently. "That's my job, to collect all the stories that involve the unicorns."

"Not only to collect them," said Lightfoot sharply. "To record them and make them accessible. You'll have the story in good time. Right now, *we* need the story behind what is happening to this child. Cara, show him the amulet."

Rising, Cara pulled the amulet from beneath her T-shirt. Lifting the chain over her head, she carried it to Grimwold. He gasped. "One of the Queen's Five," he muttered as he examined it. After a moment he looked up at her. "Did Ivy give this to you?"

Cara nodded.

"*Why?*"

She took a breath, then told him what had happened the evening she and her grandmother had been pursued into St. Christopher's. Grimwold made notes as she spoke, his pen scratching across the paper. When she was finished, he picked up the amulet and let it dangle from his fingertips. He stared at it with an expression that Cara found strange and terrible. After a moment he looked at Lightfoot and said, "I fear that the Hunters have returned."

"Who are the Hunters?" asked Cara.

Before Grimwold could answer, Lightfoot came to stand beside her. She placed her hand on his shoulder.

"Use the common tongue," the unicorn said to Grimwold. "The others must hear this as well."

To Cara's shock, she felt an undertone of fear in Lightfoot's message, a fear so strong it frightened her as well.

"Certainly," said Grimwold, "though much of it will be things that you already know."

"That is all right," said Lightfoot. "Cara, come sit with me while Grimwold tells of what has been, of the enemy that drove us from Earth so long ago."

They returned to the purple rug. Cara knelt with her hand on Lightfoot's neck and stared at the old man expectantly. The Dimblethum growled and shifted in his seat. The Squijum left off his explorations and returned to Thomas's lap.

Looking directly at Cara, Grimwold said, "This is the story of the hunting of the unicorns, and how it began. At least, it is the short version of that tale, for I could tell it in a way that would take many evenings and let you know the deeds of many heroes, both human and unicorn."

He lowered his voice, speaking more intensely. "Their sacrifices led to the creation of the first door between Earth and Luster, the path the unicorns followed to safety and freedom. This is the story behind that story, the story from which springs all other stories gathered here in the Unicorn Chronicles, all other songs sung on this world. It is a tale woven from greed and loss, lies and truth, bravery and sacrifice, ending and beginning."

As Grimwold continued, Cara felt herself moving into the trance of the story. The power of his telling brought the tale to life inside her, drawing her back to a time long gone. . . .

"Back in the morning of your world [said Grimwold] when things were sweeter rougher stranger cleaner and more savage than they are today, the unicorns came forth. No one knows from whence they came. No one knows why. They just were. Their numbers were few, as if the world could only hold so much of their magic. And magic they were, for in their horns, in their hooves, in their very *being*, they carried the power to transform things.

"At first even the unicorns did not know the extent of their powers. But as time went on they found that they could clear water, heal wounds, quicken growth.

"In that early time the unicorns lived in harmony

with the world, bringing it sweetness and guarding some of the small animals for whom they took a fondness. They gathered much wisdom, which they stored in their heads, as they had no means of writing it down. Of course, in the newness of the world, there was less to know, and among them the unicorns could hold all that they had learned. Because they can communicate so easily, the knowledge was accessible to all.

"Eventually another creature came to power. That was man. And though your species has many virtues, child, there is a strain of savagery running through it that has driven much of the best and most beautiful that your world once offered into extinction, or — as in the case of the unicorns — exile."

The Dimblethum growled softly, as if remembering some old anger. Grimwold nodded toward him, acknowledging his right to complain, then continued his story.

"Man hunted. He hunted for food, for skins to warm himself and his family, even for sport. But he did not hunt the unicorns.

"Now death comes for all things, even unicorns, though they are remarkably long-lived. When the first of their kind died, a great mourning overtook the unicorns. The twelve oldest came to her body and with their horns changed her flesh to soil, her bones to water, her mane and tail to flowers. But they could not change her horn, for it was too powerful. The horn stayed as it was.

"From its perfect beauty flowed inestimable tragedy."

Cara felt Lightfoot shiver.

"A man found the horn and brought it back to his people," continued Grimwold. "But to make himself seem braver and more honorable, he did a dishonorable thing. He told a great lie about the ferocity of the unicorn from which he had taken the horn, claiming that she had attacked him in the wood, and that he had battled it to the death. In that falsehood lay the seeds of the tragedy that followed."

15

A TALE OF BLOOD
AND SORROW

"The story of the fierce unicorn was repeated often, and the wide-eyed children who heard it had no reason to disbelieve. Yet the power of the horn was such that it began to transform the man who had found it. The lies retreated from his heart and with them the need to feel higher than his fellows. Slowly he learned to use the horn to heal, to help, to protect.

"Eventually he even tried to take back the story of how he had obtained it. But lies have a life of their own and are harder to kill than either men or unicorns.

"People began to come from great distances to be touched by the horn. But since the horn was no longer part of a living being, the magic it held could not be replenished. Over the years its power was slowly drained, until at last it was empty of everything save beauty.

"Now, even before the horn had lost its magic, other men had desired one of their own, longing for the power and prestige that would come to whoever possessed such a miracle. With the horn drained, the dream of owning one became even more intense, for no healer who walked the Earth at that time had the certain power of the horn.

"Even so, only the bravest went seeking unicorns. For while the horn had lost its power, the lie told by its finder had grown in strength. Men now believed the story of fierce and deadly unicorns as if they had experienced it firsthand."

"We can be fierce if need be," said Lightfoot proudly.

"It is something you learned in the terrible years that followed," replied Grimwold. He paused, then turning to Cara said, "It started with a girl about your age. She was the child of a great hunter, a man both ferocious and determined. His wife had died giving birth to the girl, and thereafter he had lived alone in the forest with only his child for company. He called her 'Beloved,' for he had given all his heart to her.

"Beloved fell ill. On the first day of her sickness, the hunter tended her himself. But on the second day she was much worse, so he went to the village and brought the healer back to their forest home.

"But the healer could do nothing. 'Alas that we no longer have a unicorn's horn,' he muttered as he left the hut.

"The father's quick ears heard these words.

"With each passing day, Beloved's condition grew worse. On the third day after the healer's failure, the hunter said to himself. 'I shall find me a unicorn. I care not for its ferocity. I care not for my own life, should Beloved die. I will hunt, and I will find, and I will tear the horn from its head.' "

Cara could feel Lightfoot shudder. Horrible as the story was, she wondered what it would be like to have a father who loved her like that.

"Such was the hunter's love for his daughter," continued Grimwold, "that he never questioned whether his vow was good or evil, wise or foolish. The child alone was in his mind and his heart as he went a-hunting.

"His quest carried him far and wide. But each night he returned to the cottage to care for Beloved and tend her needs. He was a solitary man, and even had he known someone who could come and help with the child, he would not have known how to ask. Alas, each night when he returned to the cottage, the child was worse than when he had left her. The days drew on. She begged him to stay by her side until she died, as she was sure now that she must do.

"But the hunter had become obsessed with the quest for the horn. Wild-eyed, he refused his daughter's pleas and instead strapped her to his back and carried her with him on his hunt. It was not hard, for her illness had wasted her and she weighed but little. Nor did she complain, for she loved her father and longed to be with him."

Cara sighed, thinking what that must have been like. Grimwold glanced at her, but made no comment.

"In the forest," he continued, "the hunter left Beloved in a place he deemed safe, a place his hunter's skills told him was not visited by great cats or other fierce beasts. Then he began circling out, searching for a unicorn, haunted by the fear that he would come back and find his daughter dead from her illness.

"Late that afternoon a breeze caught and carried Beloved's scent to a unicorn named Whiteling, who was wading in a stream some miles away. The smell of her pain and need, of her approaching death, touched his heart. He began seeking the child even as her father was returning from his hunt.

"Whiteling reached the clearing first. He did not enter at once, for unicorns were wary around humans. But something about the child drew him in — her innocence, perhaps, or her pain, or simply the knowledge that he could heal her. Silently, on feet that could cross a field of flowers without crushing a petal, he began to walk toward the girl.

"She lay equally silent, eyes closed, breathing shallow.

"Lowering his horn, Whiteling pointed it at Beloved's breast even as her father drew near the clearing. The hunter's heart filled with terror when he saw the very beast he had been seeking, the beast he had been taught from boyhood was ferocious beyond all others, heading for his daughter. He reached into his quiver, drew forth an arrow, nocked it to his bow."

Cara drew a sharp breath. She could feel Lightfoot grow tense beside her.

"The unicorn bent to heal the child. The father loosed his arrow. It flew straight and true, piercing Whiteling's heart at the very moment that his horn pierced the heart of the ailing girl. He screamed and reared, trumpeting his pain.

"Bellowing with rage, the hunter raced into the clearing. Whiteling turned on him and the two began to fight.

"The battle was brief, but bloody. When it was done, both man and beast lay dead on the forest floor. The only living thing in the clearing was Beloved, who had watched the tragedy through wide and terrified eyes.

"Whiteling had cured her illness. Yet her heart was filled with an icy pain. Here is the reason: When the arrow struck Whiteling, he had snapped up his head so fast that the tip of his horn caught beneath Beloved's breastbone and broke off there. That piece of horn was now lodged in her heart, which was doomed to be forever wounded, forever healing, both in the same instant."

Cara put her hand to her chest, trying to imagine the feeling.

"Though it took seven days, Beloved buried her father in that clearing, digging his grave with the broken horn that she had hacked from Whiteling's head with her father's knife. When she was done, she stood atop her father's grave. Holding the alicorn with both hands, afire with pain, she swore that she and her children, her children's children, and all the generations that followed would be foes of all unicorns, and hunt them and kill them until the last days and the ends of the Earth.

"Only then did she return to the cottage that she had shared with her father. Eventually she found another hunter and married him, and gave birth to seven sons. Each son was trained in the ways of the wood, and the trail, and the hunt; each sought unicorns to slay, which they did by acting out their mother's story and placing a young woman in the woods.

"The hunters believed this lured the unicorns because they wanted to savage the innocent girl. But the real reason was even stranger. In the moment of Whiteling's death, the unicorns had been taken by a kind of madness. He was the first of their kind to be killed, and each unicorn had felt the moment when his horn had been broken. Each had seen, for an instant, through his eyes. And what they had seen was a young girl, lost in pain and fear. These two things, the girl and the broken horn, were fused in their minds, and they sought ever and again to find the missing bit of horn and to bring peace to young maidens — usually to the unicorns' own grief and sorrow.

"The sons of Beloved grew old and died. But Beloved herself did not, for the piece of horn lodged in her heart kept her alive, ever wounded, ever healing. Grandsons she had, and great-grandsons after that. And as is true for many families in your world, they came to be known by what they did; they came to be called the Hunters. Of course, many are known as Hunter who do not come from this clan. And there are many born to the clan who do not know its true past. But from each generation Beloved herself selects a handful to carry on the family quest: to seek and to slay unicorns."

Grimwold paused and shook himself, as if coming out of a trance. Looking directly at Cara, he said, "After a time the unicorns opened the first door to Luster. They fled here to have a world of their own, where they would be safe from the Hunters, and the curse of Beloved. But that is another story and a long one at that. What you need to know now is that for centuries the Hunters sought to enter this world, in order to carry on their quest for revenge. Then something happened, and for a long time we did not hear anything of them. We even dared hope that the line had finally died out or given up.

"We were wrong. I am sure that the man chasing you is one of the clan. His goal is to gain the amulet so he can open a door to Luster to others of his kind. Perhaps the Hunter and the delvers are in league. Even if they are not, should the delvers succeed in opening a door, the Hunters will be ready. The slaughter will begin again."

Cara felt a cold terror in her heart — partly because of what Grimwold had just said, but even more because she finally knew the identity of the man who had chased her grandmother and her into St. Christopher's.

She knew, but she dare not tell.

16

THE SCRYING POOL

ightfoot shifted uneasily beside her. "I do not like that story," he said. "It makes me unhappy."

"I did not tell it to brighten your day," replied Grimwold sharply. "I told it because you have become part of it."

"But how do you know that the man who is chasing us is a Hunter?" asked Cara.

"Who else would seek the amulet? Someone else might have heard of it, I suppose. But when you add the amulet to the tracking, the pursuit of you and your grandmother, it smacks to me of Hunters."

"Do you think he would have hurt my grandmother?" she asked.

Grimwold frowned. "It is hard to say. Though their quarrel is only with the unicorns, they can be ruthless in their pursuit."

Cara groaned. "What should we do now?"

"Let us try to contact the Queen," said Grimwold.

"How do we do that?"

"Through the scrying pool," he said.

Cara wrinkled her brow. "What's that?"

Rather than answering directly, Grimwold said, "Follow me." He rose and led them to a door in the side of the Story Room.

When they stepped through it, Cara caught her breath in wonder and desire. If the Story Room was the best room she had ever seen, the *contents* of this next room were — especially for someone who could think of little better than to live in a library — overwhelming.

It was a room of books, shelves and racks and rows of books. And every one of them looked old and mysterious, as if it held secrets too fascinating to be put in more modern-looking volumes. Scrolls there were as well, and four or five polished wooden stands where thick books lay open with ribbons marking their pages.

"What are all these?" she asked.

"The Unicorn Chronicles," replied Grimwold. "They hold the history of all that has happened since the unicorns first came to Luster."

"But where did they come from?"

Grimwold shrugged. "From me. From the unicorns. The unicorns bring me their stories and I write them down."

"You wrote all of these?" she asked in astonishment.

"I have been here a long time," he replied, as if that explained everything. "And please remember, I do not invent the stories — I simply record what the unicorns tell me. You will be in here, too, before long, because you are part of one of their stories as well. Though should things go wrong with this one . . ." He trailed off, as if the possibility was too horrible to contemplate.

"But where do the things to make them come from?" she asked. "The paper and the ink and the pens and — well, *everything*!" she finished, waving her hands in a gesture that took in not only this room, but the one they had just left, and the hall beyond that, with its paintings and portraits.

"You are not the only human who has come to Luster," said Lightfoot gently.

"More's the pity," growled the Dimblethum.

They had reached an arched door at the far side of the library. Grimwold paused with his hand on the thick metal latch and said, "The unicorns have lived here for a long time now. In the time since they first opened the passage to this world, humans have stumbled, fallen, lied, cheated, bought, magicked, and hoped their way here. Whether or not they are allowed to stay is a complicated matter. But any who do are expected to serve the Queen. My job is to chronicle the days of the unicorns. Others there are who make paper, who bind books, who fashion things of beauty and worth."

"Or fix things," said Thomas cheerfully.

"Where do the other humans live?" Cara asked.

"Here and there," said Grimwold with a shrug. "Usually in clumps and clusters, the way humans tend to, though some are solitary, and live in cottages built far from the beaten path."

"Some just travel," added Thomas.

Grimwold, who clearly did not like to be interrupted, shot him a nasty look. Thomas took out one of his watches and looked at it as if it contained important information.

"The people who find their way here often tend to be loners," continued the dwarf. "So some do not live any place at all but wander the paths of Luster, doing errands when the Queen summons them."

Thomas smiled and nodded.

Grimwold snorted and opened the door he had been holding. The others followed him out of the library into a cave that had been left in its natural form. In its center three tripods supported small cauldrons filled with something that glowed a soft orange. By this dim light, Cara saw irregular stone walls, and a scattering of stalactites and stalagmites. Centered between the tripods was a stone basin much like the one that had held the cold fire in the main cavern. However, rather than fire, this basin held dark, cold-looking water.

"The scrying pool," said Grimwold. Then he ordered Lightfoot to dip his horn in the basin.

The unicorn nodded and stepped forward. When he bent his horn to the water, silver shimmered across the surface of the basin.

"Stand beside me," the dwarf said to Cara, positioning himself at the edge of the basin.

She stood where he indicated.

"Look into the water."

Again, she complied. To her surprise, the surface of the water began to shimmer. Slowly an image began to appear. It was not her reflection, nor a reflection of the cavern, but an entirely different place, green and pleasant looking.

"Summerhaven," said Lightfoot, who was standing behind them. He backed up a step or two. "I'd just as soon you not tell the Queen I'm here," he said to Grimwold.

The Squijum had jumped onto the rim of the basin and was looking into the pool with fascination. "Very much good pretty," he said, reaching out to touch the water.

Cara expected Grimwold to snap at the little creature and shoo him away. But before the dwarf could move, the water roiled and darkened.

"Yikes!" squealed the Squijum, leaping onto Cara's shoulder.

Grimwold cursed in astonishment.

"What is it?" asked Cara. "What's happening?"

"Something has interfered with the connection," he said. He shivered, and the look in his eyes sent a chill down Cara's spine as well. "This has never happened before," he continued. "The pool is a powerful magic. The Queen herself set it up for me. I cannot imagine what could —"

"Look!" said Lightfoot.

All eyes turned to the pool. A message had appeared on the surface of the troubled water, written in large, flowing letters, as if from some great pen.

It said: "Surrender the Amulet."

It was signed, *"Beloved."*

17

UPWARD

"You must leave this place at once," said Grimwold.

"Why?" asked Cara, who was still shaking with the shock of the message.

"Because she knows that you are here."

They had returned to Grimwold's writing room. The old dwarf was pacing back and forth in front of the fireplace, chewing his lips.

"This is worse than anything I could have imagined," he said. "Beloved has not been heard from for years. I had even dared hope she might finally have died. Now you arrive with this amulet, a Hunter hot on your trail, and the ancient enemy tracing your path. I do not like this. I do not like it at all."

Cara shifted nervously in her seat, feeling vaguely

guilty, as if the entire situation were somehow her fault. She started to say something, then stopped herself.

"Why not destroy the amulet?" growled the Dimblethum.

"Be my guest," said Grimwold. Gesturing toward the fireplace, he nodded to Cara and said, "Throw it in, if you wish."

"Won't the Queen be angry?" she asked, at the same time wondering what such an action would mean for her own chances of getting home.

Grimwold shrugged. "Probably not. I suggested it merely for the sake of demonstration. If you throw it in, it will not melt. Hammer it, it will not bend. To destroy it would take a magic more powerful than can be found in this cave."

"Things that cannot be broken are generally a bad idea," said Thomas.

Cara shivered. "Where is Beloved now?" she asked. "On Earth — or here in Luster?"

"I do not know," said Grimwold, "though I dearly hope that she is still in your world. Bad enough that she has some agent in this world — probably one of the Hunters, which is even worse — without her being here herself."

"If she knows where we are, knows to send a message here saying she wants the amulet, isn't it likely that she will have someone in place to steal it as soon as we leave here?" asked Lightfoot.

"Absolutely," replied Grimwold. "Which is why

you must leave in secret. I will take you to one of the back tunnels. It will let you out in Firethroat's territory."

"Yikes!" squealed the Squijum.

"She should not bother you," said Grimwold. "I have long since made peace with the Great Lady. In fact, she herself suggested this emergency exit."

"What do we do after we leave?" asked Cara.

"Make for Summerhaven and the Queen with all the speed that you can manage. I had hoped to summon help, an honor guard to take you and the amulet safely to court. Now you will need to travel as swiftly and secretly as you can. *The amulet must not fall into Beloved's hands! If it does . . .*"

He shook his head, as if the magnitude of the catastrophe was beyond his power to describe.

The trip through the tunnels was longer than Cara had expected, mostly because it had not occurred to her that Grimwold could have such a lengthy passage underground. They traveled first through a corridor lined with wood, then for a long way through natural rock, crossing underground streams, traversing caves so huge she wasn't sure they would find the other side, and narrow places so small the Dimblethum could barely squeeze through them. Finally they left the caverns and entered an earthen tunnel supported by beams.

Man-made! Cara thought to herself, then realized

that here on Luster *handmade* was the most she could say and be sure that she had the truth.

The Squijum rode on her shoulder for most of the journey, nervously crooning nonsense syllables in her ear. His fluffy tail curled around her neck felt as friendly and safe as the stuffed animals that lined her bed at home.

Home. The thought nearly stopped her in her tracks. She could not think of home without thinking of her grandmother. And she could not think of her grandmother without a pang of fear, wondering what had happened to her in the tower of St. Christopher's — though now that she knew *who* had chased them there, she was even more confused.

Aside from the Squijum's chatter, they traveled in silence. Once or twice Lightfoot made a point of stepping beside her. When she put her hand on his shoulder he thought to her, "I just wanted to see if you were all right."

Eventually they reached a set of five earthen steps. The steps led up to a wooden door. The door slanted toward them. The angle was so sharp that when Cara pressed her forehead to the door, its base was still some five feet ahead of her, level with her knees.

Grimwold said something to the Dimblethum. The creature put a pawlike hand on Cara's shoulder to draw her back. Stepping past her, he pressed his shoulder against the door. It opened into twilight, revealing a sky just starting to blossom with stars.

Cara now saw that the reason for the door's angle was that it was set in the side of a hill. Once outside, she saw that the door's exterior had been disguised with grass and wildflowers and rocks that she guessed must somehow have been glued in place. (Or, she realized, held there by some sort of magic.)

Grimwold pointed ahead of them and began to speak to Lightfoot — giving the unicorn directions, Cara assumed.

The dwarf turned to her. "It was a great pleasure to meet you, Miss Cara," he said with such obvious sincerity that she suddenly felt somehow more at home here. "Not all stories are good, not all endings are happy. May your story, on which may ride the fate of us all, be both good and happy. Give my regards to the Queen, and to your grandmother, if you are lucky enough to see them."

"I will," replied Cara, somewhat confused by the combination of gloom and hope in the dwarf's words.

Grimwold turned and stepped into the hillside. When he closed the door, it was almost as if he had never been there.

The Dimblethum made some growling noises. Cara put her hand on Lightfoot's shoulder, too late to understand the meaning of the growls, but in time to catch the unicorn's response, which was basically, "As fast as possible." Turning his attention to Cara, he added, "Would you like to ride?"

She scrambled onto his back, twining her fingers

in the spun silk of his mane, pressing her knees to his sides. No need to urge this steed to speed, or for a bridle to guide him. She merely held on as he sped through the grassland, straight into the domain of the dragon.

The Squijum and the Dimblethum traveled beside them, the Dimblethum usually on his hind legs, but occasionally dropping to all fours. Thomas ambled along behind, seeming not to hurry, yet never falling very far back.

They were nearing the foothills. A full moon had risen, painting the entire landscape with silver light. Suddenly the Squijum screeched and leaped onto the Dimblethum's back. "Look see look look look!" he cried, pointing moonward.

Cara looked up and gasped. Dark against the darkness of the night, Firethroat was flying. She crossed the moon once, and then again, her great and terrifying shape stark against the silver orb. On the second pass Cara realized that the dragon was getting closer. For a moment she tried to convince herself it was mere coincidence, but too soon it became obvious that Firethroat was heading straight for them.

"Run!" she cried to Lightfoot, forgetting that her spoken words carried no meaning for him. It didn't make any difference; the thought was so strong in her that she didn't need to try to send it to him. It flowed from her in a wash of panic so powerful that he reared back and pawed at the air.

Cara slid from his back, landing with a thump on the soft grass. Part of her remembered Lightfoot's warning that to run would only anger the dragon. But with that great, bat-winged form swooping toward them from the darkness, such advice was hard to heed. Scrambling to her feet, she shot off through the grass. Something grabbed her neck. She screamed before she realized it was the Squijum, who had leaped onto her shoulders and was gibbering with a fear that matched her own.

To her astonishment, Lightfoot held his ground. He stood in the moonlight, wind streaming through his mane, staring up at the dragon as if daring her to take him.

Cara caught her breath as Firethroat swooped low above the unicorn. The creature was enormous, her head the size of a car, the span of her wings wider than a house. Lightfoot, even the Dimblethum, suddenly seemed tiny in comparison.

Raising her head, the dragon shot a column of fire into the sky. Then she flapped those enormous wings a single time and swooped over Cara. Closing her right claw around the girl, the dragon turned and headed upward.

Cara screamed and kicked as she was lifted from the ground. But the talon that had closed around her waist was like a band of iron: smooth, hard, unbreakable. Her stomach lurched as the world fell away below her. Her legs dangled uselessly, and with nothing supporting her she was terrified that she would fall. At the same time, irrationally she was struggling to escape the dragon's grip, even though success would have sent her tumbling to the ground, increasingly far below. The Squijum, which still clung to her neck, was screeching in terror.

The dragon wheeled, and, almost as an afterthought, veered toward the ground again and snatched up Lightfoot with her other claw. Then into the air she rose. As Cara watched the land fall away below them she spotted Thomas and the Dimblethum, the latter roaring and stretching his fists toward the sky. Slowly they dwindled, until they were nothing but specks.

The dragon flew on.

18

IN FIRETHROAT'S CAVE

irethroat flew higher and higher, until Cara felt that all of Luster was spread below them, a world of forests and plains, broad swamps and great rivers. In the distance, sparkling in the moonlight, a vast body of water stretched on farther than she could see, some huge lake, or inland sea, perhaps even an ocean.

Cara looked to her right, where Lightfoot dangled from the dragon's other claw, which held him around the middle. She wanted to speak to him, but it was impossible without direct contact.

To her surprise she was quite warm. She soon realized that the warmth emanated from the dragon's belly.

The Squijum, muttering in terror, had burrowed

between her body and Firethroat's claw. Cara worried that he might tickle the dragon into dropping them. But once he stopped squirming she realized it was almost comforting to have the little fellow snuggled against her.

They were above the mountains now, rising higher with the beating of Firethroat's great wings. The land below them, marked with cliffs and crags, grew wilder and rockier the higher they flew.

Was Firethroat planning to eat them? Perhaps she was simply going to drop them from some great height. Why was she angry with them? Simply for invading her territory? Or had they committed some other crime? She remembered Lightfoot saying that Firethroat had no patience with fools. She also remembered Grandmother Morris asking if anyone could be sure that he was not a fool.

The dragon banked to the right, and Cara felt dizzy as the world tipped beneath her. Then they swooped toward the side of a mountain. For a moment her heart leaped with new fear as she thought the dragon was going to dash them against the cliffs. At the last moment Firethroat flapped her wings just enough to lift them above the edge of the cliff onto a broad shelf of rock that fronted an enormous cave. After depositing them on the flat surface, the dragon settled in herself. She had no need to fear her prey would run away; the only possible routes were over the cliff or past herself.

On wobbly legs Cara stumbled to Lightfoot and

placed a hand on his shoulder. *Are you all right?* she thought.

Better than I'm likely to be in a few moments, he replied.

Suddenly the Squijum bolted from her shoulder and attempted to race past Firethroat. The dragon put out one enormous claw to block the little creature's path. Squeaking with distress, the Squijum scrambled over the claw and disappeared on the other side.

Firethroat made a dangerous noise deep in her throat. Cara wondered if the dragon would now cook her and Lightfoot out of mere annoyance. Instead, Firethroat simply looked at them, which was almost as frightening. Indeed, after a few moments in the dragon's gaze Cara felt as if she *had* been cooked.

The dragon did not move. After a time Cara forced herself to look back. She realized, with some surprise, that Firethroat was quite beautiful — if *astonishingly* large. The eyes that stared at her were nearly the size of her bedroom windows. Tendrils of smoke curled from flared nostrils so big that you could easily have roasted a turkey in either of them.

Reddish scales that had the appearance of burnished metal covered her massive head. Her long neck disappeared into the darkness of the cave, though the end of her tail looped forward again so that its pointed tip lay only a few feet from Cara. Finally Firethroat said, "So. You are the one for whom I have suffered so much humiliation."

Though Cara had her hand on Lightfoot's shoulder, she didn't need the connection to understand the dragon. The beast spoke in perfect English!

Cara was so surprised that she ignored the dragon's strange statement and asked, "How do you know my language?"

"Each species has its gifts," replied Firethroat. "The unicorns are healers. You humans have your hands and your inventive brains, always thinking of new things to make. We dragons have — among other things — the gift of tongues."

This time Cara understood that the dragon was whispering, and realized that if she spoke with her full voice it would probably blow them off the mountainside.

Cara paused. The next question felt dangerous, as if once asked, it would open the door to a problem that could overwhelm them all. And yet there was no way back, no choice but to ask it. Realizing that the very presence of the dragon seemed to demand that she speak formally, she asked, "How have I brought humiliation upon you?"

Firethroat made that terrifying noise in her throat again. The smoke curling from her nose became thicker, darker.

"I am very old," she whispered. "It has been many hundreds of years since anyone dared trifle with me. Yet two days ago a man came to this cave while I was out flying. Few men there are in Luster and even fewer that would dare come here. This man dared to come, and much more. He went to the store of my treasures, which no man on Luster has ever done. Worse still, he disturbed that store, rummaging through it for the greatest prize of the lot, which he stole from me, to my shame and humiliation, and to your great sorrow."

"What was it that he stole?" asked Cara nervously.

Firethroat snorted twice. Little gouts of flame licked around the edges of her enormous nostrils.

"One does not become as old as I am without being wily as well. Before I came to Luster, many a man wished to kill me for the sake of impressing some fair lady whose span of days would be no more to me than the mayfly is to you. Most of these men were easily defeated. Yet I knew the day would come when some man would catch me while I was contemplating the poetry of the sky and the messages written in the clouds and not thinking about men and their treachery. I knew that in that moment I would die.

"So I wove a great enchantment. It took the help of many, for many were the magic makers, witches and wizards and sorcerers of all sorts, who were in my debt. Together we took my heart from my body and placed it in a golden casket. So long as my heart was in that casket it was safe, and I could not be harmed.

"The man who came to my cave yesterday did what no man has ever dared to do, or even thought of doing. He stole my heart, and told me he would not return it until I did his bidding."

The dragon closed her eyes for a moment, and Cara felt a flash of pain and embarrassment so overwhelming that she almost wished she could fling herself from the cliff.

"He who holds the casket holds my heart. He who holds my heart, holds me, and can command me as he wishes. This was the price of the magic, the geas that is laid on me. I have no quarrel with you or your companions. But the man who holds my heart asked for you, and I had no choice but to obey."

"Who is it that holds your heart?" asked Cara, sickeningly sure that she knew the answer already.

Firethroat did not speak. From behind the dragon a clear strong voice said, "I do."

Footsteps echoed across the floor of the cave as the man stepped from the darkness, stood beside the dragon's head. He was tall, with red hair. His eyes were dark, his face hard and lean. In his hands he held a large casket made of gold. Placing it on the ground, he put one foot on top of it, triumphant, confident.

Firethroat groaned.

Cara's heart was beating like a captured bird, and something thick seemed to have lodged itself in her throat.

The man turned to her and spoke. She did not

need to hear his voice to know he was the man who had pursued her into St. Christopher's — to know he was that man, and so much more.

"Hello, Cara," he said.

She closed her eyes and swallowed. Then she whispered, "Hello . . . Daddy."

19

FAMILY MATTERS

Lightfoot cried out and flinched away from her as if he had been burned. In the instant before he moved, she could sense the feeling of betrayal that washed through him. Firethroat closed her eyes, like someone pulling the shade over a window. It was a gesture of understanding, of resignation, of defeat.

As for Cara, her heart was running wild with so many emotions that she simply could not move. She stared at the man she had longed for for so long, a deep and indefinable ache stretching through her body. At last she saw the face for the voice in the tower, the secret face that had haunted her dreams since she entered Luster.

Trying to keep her voice from breaking, she whispered, "Where have you been all this time, Daddy?"

"I have been doing the family's business. *Your* business, Cara Diana. I have been guarding our world against the intrusion of murdering beasts like the one that stands beside you. Even more, I have been seeking a way to enter *this* world, so that the hunt can end at last, and we can rest."

"Is that why you left me?" she asked. It was hard to force the words past the pain in her throat.

He shook his head sadly. "I never left you, sweetheart."

She blinked in astonishment, her heart leaping. Of all the things he might have said, this is the one she would most have longed to hear. But she did not know what to make of it, whether to trust it.

"What do you mean?" she asked at last.

"I didn't leave you. Your grandmother stole you from me."

A wave of coldness, filled with terror and sorrow, washed over her. "What do you mean?" she asked again weakly.

He sighed. "Do you remember that once when you were little you became very sick?"

She nodded. "And a unicorn came and healed me. I stopped believing that for a long time. But now I know it's true."

"Your grandmother summoned that unicorn," said her father. "She was always a friend of unicorns, and they would do as she asked. But in saving you, she had created a problem." He sighed. "That problem was me. I swear I do not know why I fell in love with your mother, Cara, don't know if Grandmother Beloved set me on that path to get to your grandmother. I did know, though I never understood why, that it broke Ivy Morris's heart when her daughter married a man named Hunter." He sighed again. "At the time I didn't know the secret of our family. But after the unicorn had come, Beloved called me, and I was initiated. You have to believe me, Cara. I did not abandon you. Your grandmother took you from me because she was afraid I would use you to get at the unicorns."

"And would you have?" she asked.

Her father hesitated. "Yes," he said at last.

Cara felt as if her heart was being torn in half. How could her grandmother have done such a thing to her? Yet how could she not? She had been to Luster, been a friend of unicorns. Knowing what her son-in-law's family would do if they could enter this world, she would have been forced to take action.

Cara wondered whose pain had been greater — her own or her grandmother's?

Or maybe even her father's?

She wondered if there was anyone in the world that she could trust.

She wondered if the hurt would ever go away again.

"Is Grandmother Morris all right?" she asked. "Did you hurt her in the tower?"

The question caused her father's face to twist with

pain. "What kind of a man do you think I am?" he cried.

"I don't know!" she screamed. "I don't know anything anymore!"

A horrible silence filled the cave.

Ian Hunter knelt, careful to keep one knee on the casket, and looked directly at her. Spreading his arms to welcome her in, he whispered, "I have missed you so, my Cara, my dear one." His eyes were large and dark with sorrow. "You don't know yet what it means to be part of our family, Cara, don't know the burden we carry, protecting Earth from his kind. Since you fell through here ahead of me I have been terrified that one of them would kill you before I could save you."

"Lightfoot has been kind to me," she said, confused.

"They are cunning," her father replied with a sneer. "They knew I was coming and wanted you on their side. But you were born to help bring an end to them. Give me the amulet, sweetheart. Once I have it, we can go home."

"And then what?" she asked, her voice, her body, trembling.

"Then the final hunt will begin. After a time the unicorns will be gone and our family's task will be ended. Beloved will be able to rest at last and so will I. Then you and I can be together again. You don't know how I've longed for that day, Cara, how much I regret the lost time. But Grandmother Beloved called, and I had no choice but to answer. And you — you had disappeared. I wanted to hunt for you, but first I had to be trained for our great mission. Yet I always knew that one day I would find you again."

Cara closed her eyes, imagining it.

"What about Mommy?" she asked.

She had meant to say, "my mother," but it had been eight years since she had last seen the woman she called by that name, and when she thought of her, thought of the night she had disappeared, it was the word "Mommy" that forced its way through her throat.

"Mommy is waiting for you," said her father.

Cara heard the dragon shift behind her, but it was a momentary noise, and then the great beast was quiet once more.

Her father held out his hand. "Bring me the amulet, Cara Diana."

Still she stood without moving, as if frozen by hearing once more the name he had called her when she was but a toddler, the name he called her when he threw her in the air, and played peekaboo, and tucked her in at night.

"Bring me the amulet," he said again, his voice strong.

Slowly she stepped forward. Raising her hands to her neck, she lifted the mended chain that held the amulet.

Lightfoot whickered, and even though she was not

connected to him, she could hear in that sound fear, and sorrow, and his sense of betrayal.

Tears in her eyes, she took another step forward, studying her father's face, uncertain if she would be able to do what she had to do.

"I'm waiting, Cara," he said, voice gentle, eyes hard.

Cara ran toward him, raising her arms as if to embrace him. But just before she reached him she stopped and threw the amulet. It soared above his head.

"What . . . ?" he cried, then he turned to scramble for it.

But the Squijum was faster; it had already caught the amulet and was racing into the darkness. Ian Hunter lunged for the little creature, then suddenly twisted back, a look of fear on his face.

He was too late. Cara had seized the golden casket that held Firethroat's heart and was backing away from him, toward the unicorn and the dragon.

"Cara!" he screamed. "What are you doing?"

She said nothing.

"Cara, give that back to me. You don't know what kind of catastrophe you could create. *Give it back to me!*"

"I'm sorry, Daddy," she said softly. "I can't do that."

"Cara, I'm your father. I demand that you give it to me."

She laughed, but it was a painful sound, a laugh that held eight years of sorrow and loss.

He spoke again, more calmly. "Cara, you are a Hunter, one of the clan. You were born to this. It is the final chapter of our story, the chance to end the hunt forever. Your blood binds you — my blood, the blood of Beloved that runs in our veins. It's family, Cara Diana, Cara Diana *Hunter*. Family. You belong to us, to Beloved."

"Family isn't blood," she said bitterly, continuing to back away. "Family is who loves you, who takes care of you."

"I wanted to take care of you!" he cried, his words pouring out in a howl of pain. "You were stolen from me!"

The sorrow in his voice pierced her, and she wanted to run to him. But she saw that even as he mourned her loss, he was judging the distance between them, preparing to leap.

She took another step back, then turned and ran.

She wanted to call on Firethroat for help, but feared that if she unleashed the dragon's wrath, the beast would destroy her father. She didn't want to destroy him, merely wanted him sent back to Earth, far from her and the unicorns. She hadn't thought further ahead than keeping the amulet out of his grasp.

His leap brought him within inches of her. She ran faster, heading for the front of the cave, uncertain where she would go after that.

"Come back here!" he roared, scrambling to his feet, sprinting after her.

Firethroat, freed from Ian Hunter's hold on her heart, was stirring.

"Don't hurt him!" cried Cara, and, because she held the dragon's heart, Firethroat was bound by her command.

Her father tackled her. They fell together, near the edge of the cliff. He would have wrenched the casket from her then, but Lightfoot trumpeted and began to pelt the man with his hooves. Hunter drew back. Then, as if invincible to the pain, he lunged forward again. Stretching his arms, he tried to tear the golden casket from his daughter's hands. Lightfoot struck his hands away just before they closed on the casket.

Cara scrambled to her feet. Her father, intent on the casket, grabbed her legs. She fell again, closer to the edge. They began to wrestle. Lightfoot bugled a warning, but it went unheeded. They rolled over once and then were gone over the edge of the cliff.

It was different from the leap from the tower of St. Christopher's. Then, she had leaped into light, with a glimmer of hope that she might come to something better. Now, she only fell, through the night in the mountains, toward not a street but a heap of snow-covered rock so far below it made the distance from tower to street seem like a baby step. She fell with no hope, only primal terror ripping through her.

Her father was near but no longer holding her. She could barely see him, falling, falling, just a few feet away. Some small part of her brain registered with interest that they were falling at the same speed, though he was so much heavier.

She had heard the old story that when someone is drowning their whole life flashes before them. But drowning would be a slow death compared to this. Their speed was breathtaking. The cliffside flashed by. She couldn't breathe, couldn't think, as she saw oblivion racing toward her and then — *Snatch!* Firethroat plucked her from the air and soared upward again.

Her father was still falling.

Cara was still clutching the casket that held Firethroat's heart. Without thinking, she commanded the dragon to do her will.

"Save him!" she screamed.

20

THREE DROPS
OF BLOOD

ara sat, trembling, at the edge of the cliff, holding the golden casket against her chest. The Squijum crouched on her shoulder, crooning nonsense into her ear. Lightfoot stood behind her. She wondered what he was thinking.

Ahead of them dawn was creeping over the mountains. Suddenly, Firethroat burst into the light, appearing as if from nowhere. Her claws were empty.

Cara and her friends scrambled back from the cliff edge as the dragon returned to her cave.

"It is done," she murmured, folding her wings.

"What did you do with him?" asked Cara nervously.

The dragon regarded her with one enormous eye.

"I returned him to Earth," she said at last. "Not an easy thing to do, I assure you. But flying between worlds is another gift that dragons possess."

"Where?" Cara asked. "Where did you leave him?"

"Someplace empty," said the dragon with maddening vagueness. "I cannot go where there are people, of course. I left him safe, dry, and alive. What he does next is up to him. I care only that he does not return to Luster."

"Thank you," said Cara. "I know it was not easy for you." Stepping forward, she placed the casket on the cave floor, not far from the dragon. "Here," she whispered, pushing it forward. "Your heart is your own again."

She watched a great claw reach forward and draw the golden casket away.

Then the last of her strength left her, and the pain and the loss came flooding in. Turning from the dragon, from her friends, Cara bolted into the darkness at the back of the cave. When she stumbled and fell, she made no move to get up, simply lay on the floor, sobbing her grief and pain, until a welcome darkness blanketed her mind.

When she woke, it was dark again. The only light came from a sprinkling of stars behind her, and — to her right — a faint glow from the dragon's fiery nostrils.

Whimpering, she curled into a ball, trying to blot the memory of the previous night from her mind.

After a while she realized that someone was standing over her. Opening her eyes, she saw the glow of Lightfoot's horn. A look of gentle concern filled his eyes. He knelt beside her and she wound her arms around his neck, burying her face in the clean perfection of his mane.

"Do you hate me?" she thought.

"Why?" he asked, seeming startled by the question.

"Because I am a Hunter."

"You are Cara," he replied, "and you are not chained by blood. You are a friend of unicorns."

Though she tried to hold it in, another sob tore out of her. Clinging to Lightfoot, she wept until her lungs were sore, her face a soggy mess, whispering, "Daddy, Daddy, Daddy."

"I have no way to heal a wound such as this," said Lightfoot sadly, when she was done.

She said nothing, only tightened her grip on him, holding him as if she were tottering on the edge of an abyss far deeper and more terrifying than the one from which Firethroat had saved her.

"Are you all right?" he asked after a while.

She shook her head. "How can I be all right? I missed him so much for so long. And then . . ."

"Family ties are strange," he replied. "I have thought about them often, but never — "

He was interrupted by the Squijum. The little creature had been sitting in front of them, holding the amulet. Suddenly he darted forward and placed the golden bauble on Cara's knees. As Lightfoot stepped

150

back, the Squijum chittered something, then scrambled up Cara's arm to her shoulder and kissed her on the cheek. As if startled by his own boldness, he scampered back down and raced to the mouth of the cave, where he sat on his haunches, chattering incomprehensibly.

"I wish I could understand you," she said, half-amused, half-irritated.

"An interesting thought, young human," said Firethroat, interrupting the Squijum's chatter. "And perhaps the solution to a vexing problem."

"What problem?" asked Cara.

The dragon sighed, sending a wave of warmth in Cara's direction. "I owe you a great boon for what you have done."

"A boon?"

"It is something like a reward," explained Lightfoot. "Dragons do not like to be in anyone's debt, and you have done this lady a great service. It would be wise to accept whatever she offers with as much grace as you can manage."

"But you already saved my father," whispered Cara.

"It was commanded of me," said Firethroat. "But my heart was freely returned, and the boon must be freely given."

Cara paused, feeling the world was moving too fast for her. After a moment she said, "I would be most grateful to accept your boon, Lady Firethroat."

The dragon made a sound of approval. "Come with me," she said. "I would prefer to do this in private."

Cara followed Firethroat deep into the cave, then into a separate chamber. Here the darkness was complete, save for the dim light that came from the dragon's nostrils. Suddenly, Firethroat opened her mouth and shot forth a brief gout of flame.

Cara gasped in wonder, for at once the chamber came to life with a thousand colors, as piles of gold and jewels reflected back the burst of flame. For a moment Cara thought the purpose of the flame had been to show her what was in the room. She wondered if this was to be Firethroat's boon, some piece of fabulous treasure.

She was wrong, on both counts. Firethroat had used her flame to light a torch mounted in the wall. Now its low, flickering light danced on the gems, some as big as Cara's fist, that littered the floor.

The dragon cast her eye over a pile, then reached into it and pulled forth a jeweled chalice. "This should do," she said, passing it to Cara.

"Thank you."

The dragon chuckled. "That is not the boon."

Cara blinked.

"You didn't *want* it to be the boon, did you?" asked Firethroat.

She shook her head, hoping she wasn't getting herself into more trouble.

Firethroat stared at her. "You held my heart in your hands and returned it to me, when you could have made me your slave."

Cara shivered. The thought had never occurred to her. She found it repulsive.

"I want you to understand the granting of this boon," said the dragon. "This is only the third time in more thousands of years than I care to remember that I have done this for a human. Come here — step close."

Hesitant, nervous, Cara did as the dragon asked. As she watched, Firethroat ran the first talon of her right front foot up and down the scales of her neck.

"Here!" she said at last. Grasping one of the scales, she wrenched it from her neck. Blood welled from the wound, steaming hot.

"Catch it!" she ordered.

Cara held the chalice beneath Firethroat's neck. Three large drops of blood fell, steaming and smoking, into the chalice.

"Now drink them."

"What?" cried Cara.

"Drink them. *Quickly,* while they are still hot and the magic is strong."

Cara stared into the steaming chalice. Lightfoot's words about accepting the boon with grace sounded in her head. Closing her eyes, she lifted the chalice to her lips. Then she threw back her head and drank.

Fire scalded her throat, raced along her veins. The chalice fell from her hands. She closed her eyes, stiffened, nearly fell, straightened, stood firm.

"Are you all right?" asked Firethroat, not in Cara's

language, but in the ancient tongue of the dragons, a language of fire that came from deep in the belly.

And Cara *understood*.

"*This* is my boon," said Firethroat, "the best I have to offer. It is the gift of tongues, of knowledge of the languages of all creatures. Now there are none in Luster to whom you cannot speak, none to whom you must be a stranger."

"It is a great gift, and I am deeply honored," said Cara.

"Small return for the return of my heart," said Firethroat.

With a flick of her wing, she extinguished the torch. Then she led the way from the chamber.

21

THINGS BROKEN, THINGS MENDED

nce again Cara dangled from Firethroat's foot. But this time there was no fear, only wonder, as — safely wrapped in the dragon's claw — she looked out on the world spread wide below them.

Firethroat had agreed to return Cara, Lightfoot, and the Squijum to the place from which she had first snatched them, with the hope that they might be able to rejoin Thomas and the Dimblethum and continue their journey.

"I would take you all the way to Summerhaven," the dragon had said, "but even I cannot fly that far carrying both a unicorn and a human."

They had discussed the matter for a while, Cara joying in her ability to talk to her friends with ease and freedom. Finally they had decided that their wisest course would be to return to Grimwold's Cavern and try once more to contact the Queen.

"After all," said Lightfoot, "with the Hunter gone, Beloved's connection to this world may be severed."

He paused for a moment when he noticed the tremor of grief that twisted Cara's face at the memory he had stirred up.

"He would have destroyed us all, you know," he said softly.

She nodded. "I know. Even so . . ."

"Even so," agreed Lightfoot.

As they retraced their flight of the night before, Cara tried to pick out some of the landmarks Lightfoot had told her they would pass on the last leg of their journey to Summerhaven: the River Mallow, Chiron's Tor, Spirit Lake. Each, he said, had a story attached. And each story, of course, was stored in Grimwold's Cavern.

She longed to know them all.

It was because she was looking so hard for the landmarks that she was the first to spot the surprise awaiting them. "Look!" she cried to Lightfoot, pointing into the distance.

He stared for a moment, uncomprehending, then threw back his head and bugled his delight.

"Oh yeah much good hotcha!" burbled the Squijum, who was clinging to her neck.

*   *   *

The Dimblethum and Thomas were waiting for them when they landed.

"You're back, you're back!" roared the manbear, waving his arms in delight. Then he stood still, embarrassed at his own outburst.

"We are!" cried Cara, throwing her arms around him, at least, as far as they would reach.

He looked at her, astonished that she could speak to him. "How did . . . ?" He paused, then looked at the dragon and nodded. "The Dimblethum sees that you have a story to tell," he said.

"Well, I'm the one she'll have to tell it to," said Grimwold, stepping up beside them.

Cara was not surprised to see him there. But her attention was focused beyond him. There, standing in a rough circle, were at least a dozen unicorns, dazzling in the sunlight, dazzling in their beauty and perfection.

You should not be hunted, she thought to herself.

The largest of the unicorns stepped forward.

"It's my uncle," whispered Lightfoot. He did not sound happy.

"I bring you greetings from Queen Arabella Skydancer," said the unicorn. "She commends you on your courage and thanks you for your efforts on behalf of Luster. I am commanded to escort you and your friends to the court at Summerhaven, where you will be presented to the Queen."

"Wonderful," muttered Lightfoot bitterly. "I've

spent the last three years trying to get out of doing just that. Some reward!"

A week later, after a journey filled with marvels and wonders, Cara entered the court at Summerhaven. It was a place of green splendor, grown, not built, and at its center was a unicorn so old and so beautiful that words could not describe her. She was small and slender, as luminous as a rainbow, as fragile as a promise. You could see through her, as if you were seeing tomorrow.

To Cara's sorrow, neither Lightfoot nor the Dimblethum was with her when she entered the court. Both had come to her late in the night before they reached Summerhaven and bid her farewell.

"The Dimblethum is not really welcome there," said the manbear, putting his huge paw against her cheek, where it lay as delicately as a butterfly.

"And I am not ready to return there," said Lightfoot. "But I will see you again, I promise."

She wondered if it was true as she watched them slip into the night. She wiped a tear from her cheek.

"Chains," said the Tinker, coming up behind her. "They bind us, whether we want them to or not. But a heart without chains would have nothing to hold it, might simply blow away."

Then he held her in his arms while she wept and wept, for her father, for her grandmother, and even for the ever-wounded, ever-healing Beloved, chained to her rage for longer than anyone could imagine.

Together, Thomas, Cara, and the Squijum went to stand before the Queen. When Arabella Skydancer laid her horn across Cara's shoulder in blessing, the girl whispered, "Are you the Old One?"

"I am," said the Queen.

"Then I have a message for you. I have carried it from another world, through danger and heartbreak across this world to you. I am to tell you that the Wanderer is weary."

"Then it is time to bring her home," said the Queen. "Would you like to be the one to fetch her?"

"I would," whispered Cara. "Very much."

"Then so it shall be."

And so it was.

But that, of course, is another story altogether.

It is recorded, like all such stories, in the Unicorn Chronicles.

About the Author

Bruce Coville grew up in a rural area, around the corner from his grandparents' dairy farm. He considers himself especially lucky to have had a swamp and a forest behind his home.

His writing for children was affected by his own early reading, which included lots of pulp fiction and comic books, but also had a healthy dose of myths and legends—a taste he first developed when one of his teachers read aloud the story of Odysseus.

He has been reading fantasy ever since, and has long dreamed of creating an epic series like The Unicorn Chronicles. Bruce Coville is the author of more than 75 books for children.

He lives in an old brick house in Syracuse, New York, along with his wife, illustrator Katherine Coville, and an assortment of children.

Dangerous missions. Strange underground worlds. The journey continues...

The Unicorn Chronicles Book II:
Song of the Wanderer

New in Hardcover!

The Unicorn Chronicles Book III:
Dark Whispers

There's a mystery in every masterpiece.

In Hardcover

From the *New York Tin* bestselling author *Blue Balliett*